Joy

How to Find It
How to Keep It

by
Bruce Goettsche

Joy
by Bruce Goettsche

Printed in the United States of America

Library of Congress Control Number: 2003102353
ISBN 1-591605-14-8

Xulon Press
10640 Main Street
Suite 204
Fairfax, VA 22030
(703) 934-4411
XulonPress.com

To order additional copies, call 1-866-909-BOOK (2665).

Contents

✂

Introduction vii

1   The Foundation of Christian Joy 15

2   Finding Joy in the Difficult Times....................................27

3   Living Joyfully in Life and in Death 37

4   The Focus Needed for a Life of Joy 51

5   The Surprising Ingredient for Joyful Living......................63

6   Giving Christ His Rightful Place 75

7   Working Toward Joy...83

8   Living as Stars in the Night 93

9   Savoring The Blessings of Friendship 105

10 Overcoming the Barriers to Joy 117

11 Striving for the Best...129

12 Models: Good and Bad 139

13 Living With Anticipation 149

14 Getting Along with Others in the Church........................157

15 Getting Rid of the Sharp Edges 169

16 The Antidote to Anxiety 179

17 Learning to Think Like a Child of the King 189

18 The Secrets of Being Content 199

Acknowledgments...213

Next Dec. 16th

Introduction

❧

As a Pastor of a church for half of my life I have shared deeply with many different people. I have learned most people are carrying burdens that are quite weighty. Some have been abused, others are paralyzed by depression, and others are carrying deep wounds from divorce. There are people who have had to bury their children; battle a terminal illness; or fight the vice-grip of an addiction. Some are buried in debt. Others have plenty, but feel that their life is empty and meaningless.

I like to sit in airports or shopping malls and just watch people. At times I am stunned by the zombie-like existence that seems to characterize so many of these lives. Everyone is rushing somewhere. There is work to be done, deadlines to meet, and worlds to conquer. But I see few smiles and hear little true laughter. Joy seems to be a natural resource that is in short supply.

It would be nice to be able to say that you can find joy in ready supply in the church. Yet, in many sanctuaries the people don't look much different than those in the airport or shopping mall. There is a drudgery even among Christians that seems rather lifeless.

We have all sung about that "joy, joy, joy, joy down in our heart" but it seems to be more of a wish than a reality. We want to be joyful. In fact, some take medication to help them "feel better". Others play with illegal drugs hoping to find even a temporary sense of euphoria. But these things don't last. They cannot bring the kind of joy we long for in the depth of our being.

We all have joyful *moments*; it may be the birth of a child, a wedding day, a graduation, a special honor, a great triumph, but these are mere blips on the screen of life. It makes you wonder if a state of settled joy is really possible.

Just when you are ready to despair, someone like Dr. James Montgomery Boice comes along. Dr. Boice was a remarkable man. He was the Pastor of Tenth Presbyterian church in Philadelphia, a conference speaker, a gifted preacher and author, the speaker on the Daily Bible Study radio program, and he even wrote some hymns.

In the spring of the year 2000 Dr. Boice was diagnosed with liver cancer. The cancer appeared suddenly and took his life quickly. When Dr. Boice stood before his congregation on May 7, 2000 it was to inform them of his physical condition. As he spoke, his voice was strong and matter-of-fact. He gave them the facts (the situation was serious), he asked for their prayers, and affirmed his belief that God is in charge.

In this time that would have unraveled most people Dr. Boice joyfully affirmed God's wisdom. He confessed that although he did not understand what God was doing in his life, he declared that there was no such thing as an "accident" in the life of a child of God. Whatever God was doing, it was good. True faith, said Boice, is shown by how well we trust God in the confusing times.

In the last weeks of his life when it was apparent that treatments were not working, Dr. Boice continued to edit his books, hymns, and magazine articles. He frequently gathered his church leaders to his bedside so they could sing some of the great hymns of the faith together. Dr. Boice lived joyfully even in these devastating times. He could have been bitter or angry, but instead he rejoiced.

Dr. Boice had what I want. I want to know that kind of joy. And I think you have picked up this book because it is what you want as well. In the pages ahead we are going to pursue that goal. Our guide will be the Apostle Paul and the letter he wrote to the Philippians. The letter is just 104 verses long but in those verses joy is a recurring theme. Paul used the word "joy" in one form or another 15 times in this brief letter. The letter reveals the evidence of joy wherever you look.

What makes this letter compelling is that it was written from a jail cell. Paul is talking about joy while he sits in jail!

Most scholars believe Paul wrote this letter from a Roman prison somewhere around 61 AD. The book of Acts tells us that Paul had been arrested for instigating a riot (which he didn't do) and later was accused of committing blasphemy (because he said Jesus was Lord). He was held without a trial in Caesarea for two years (so much for due process). When an assassination plot against him was uncovered, Paul exercised his right as a Roman citizen and appealed his case to Caesar. Paul was shipped to Rome to stand trial.

When he arrived in Rome (after a harrowing voyage at sea) he was able to visit with friends while he remained under "house arrest". Like Dr. Boice, Paul rejoiced even as he endured these difficult and uncertain times. It wasn't the first time that Paul had been in jail. And it wasn't the first time he revealed joy in such circumstances.

Interestingly enough, when Paul and his friend Silas made a visit to Philippi, they were also thrown in jail. They were considered to be "trouble makers". (In those days you didn't have to have "probable cause"). While they sat in their jail cell, they read the Scriptures and held a hymn sing! Joy was Paul's companion in every circumstance.

This letter is filled with pointers that lead us to the joy that Paul and generations of others have experienced. I've tried to break these pointers down into bite-sized portions that will be easy to read. I hope you will take your time, think deeply, and apply the lessons fully.

As we look at these instructions and insights please understand that I am making the journey along with you. Too much of my life is weighted down by stress, worry, and internal churning just like you. On occasion I have caught a glimpse of joy. That glimpse has fueled my search.

I want what Dr. Boice revealed in his life. I certainly don't want to be inflicted with cancer, but if that were to happen, I'd like to face the prospect of death with joy and anticipation. I certainly don't desire the crushing burdens that some of my friends have had to face, but if they were to invade my life, I'd like to face them confident that God is good even when I don't understand what purpose the hard times have in His plan.

I begin this quest with a presupposition. I believe joy is possible *only* through a saving relationship with Jesus Christ. Joy is found in Christ. Please let me explain what I mean so that we are clear in our starting point. I believe every one of us lives our life with a God-sized hole in our heart. We long for something more than what we can see and understand. Whether we realize it or not, we are looking for God. And the great news of the Christian proclamation is that God is not hiding . . . .He is seeking us as well.

Jesus came to earth to point us to the Father. In the sermons he preached and the stories he told, he introduced us to a God who is near, and is passionately concerned about our lives. Jesus went to the cross to destroy the imposing wall of sin that made a relationship with our holy God impossible. He paid the price and absorbed the consequences for our rebellion. In His resurrection He kicked open the door of Heaven so that any who would trust Him would be able to enjoy the splendor of eternal life.

But Jesus didn't just come to earth so we could go to Heaven. He also came to earth to change our life on this side of eternity. When the angels announced the birth of Jesus, they said, "We bring you good news of great joy for all the people." (Luke 2:10). In John 15 Jesus gave his disciples a pep talk about obedience and love as they made their way to the Garden of Gethsemane where Jesus knew he would be arrested. He told his closest friends that his desire was that his "joy may be in you and your joy may be complete." In John 16:22 (part of the same conversation) Jesus said, "Now is your time of grief, but I will see you again and you will rejoice, and no one will take away your joy."

Jesus wants us to know joy in the here and now. Christianity is not just about the future; it is also about the present. Christ's message is not just for church on Sunday, it is a message that changes the way we live every day. It is not just theology; it is practical and basic instruction for joyful living in the present.

Jesus is the only one who can lead us to the joy that no one and no circumstance can take away from us. It is my hope that these words will be clear and practical. But make no mistake, you will not find joy because of my words . . . you will find joy because of your relationship with Christ.

My life has changed because of Jesus. I won't pretend that I know unceasing joy. I don't. But I am getting closer to that goal. I'm learning, and I hope through the pages of this book we can learn together. I hope we can find smiles for the hard times, confidence for the struggles, and a settled state of joy that will enrich our lives and reveal to the world the power of the gospel. I hope we can infect the world with that joy that sets Christianity apart from all the religions of the world. But to do that, we must start with Jesus.

May I be so bold as to get right to the point in the introduction to this book (just in case you don't finish)? Have you placed your confidence in Jesus? Are you still hoping you can be good enough for Heaven? Deep down inside you know you are fighting a losing battle, don't you? Jesus did for you what you cannot do for yourself. He paid for your sin and has applied His goodness to your account.

The Bible tells us that our responsibility is to "receive" the gift that Christ offers. We are to receive eternal life. But what does that mean? First, it means that you must admit that you are unable to save yourself. You must realize that you are addicted to sin and need help. You must come clean about the disease that cripples your soul. No more excuses or rationalizations. You must take responsibility for your own sin and rebellion.

Second, you must believe. You must believe that Jesus was God become man. You must believe that when He died, He died as a sinless substitute for sinful humanity. He gave His innocent life for the sin and guilt of your life. You must believe that He actually did rise from the dead (and it is good and appropriate to examine the evidence for these facts). You must believe that what He did, He did for you.

The third step is the hardest. We must take this knowledge and belief and build our life on it. True belief is not just profession; it is living on the basis of that profession. We must bet our life on the truthfulness of these things. We are to live as those who are forgiven. We are to live as those who really are headed for Heaven. We are to live confident that we are never alone. We are to live as those who are being guided by the God of the universe.

This is what separates the true believer from the spurious believer. There are lots of people who have a theoretical knowledge of Christ. They know the words. They "believe" the truths. But that knowledge never impacts their daily living. The true believer not only talks about the truth of Christianity, they build their life on that truth.

Have you done this? If you haven't, the rest of this book is going to be very frustrating for you. Please stop right now and take a fresh look at Jesus. Do you *really* believe in Him? If so, run to His arms right now. Surrender to His love and submit to His lordship and direction in your life. The words you say are really not that important. What matters is the intention of your heart. Use your own words and receive the gift of eternal life that is offered through Christ Jesus our Lord.

I'm looking forward to our journey together. Thank you for giving your time and energy to this study. It's my prayer that God will help us find the joy we've been looking for all our lives.

Someday when I get to Heaven, I am going to find Dr. Boice. I want to tell him how much his ministry and his example have impacted my life. I want to find the Apostle Paul and thank him for his letter to the Philippians (and all the others). I want to thank him for pointing the way to joy. But most of all I look forward to sitting at the feet of Jesus. I know that this is where the fullness of joy will be found.

But we don't have to wait until Heaven to know joy. Dr. Boice and the Apostle Paul proved that we could know joy in the present. To find that joy, we must cultivate a deep, honest, and abiding relationship with Jesus in the present. Paul is going to tell us how to do just that. I've tried to listen to his counsel. I pray you will too.

Study Questions
1. Who is the most "joyful" person you have ever known? How did they express their joy? What was the basis of their joy? What have you learned from them?
2. Do you think the letter to the Philippians and his comments about joy would have had less credibility if Paul had written from a computer in his plush office? Why or why not?

3. Do you agree that Jesus is the key to joy? Why?
4. What is the difference between believing IN Jesus and believing Jesus? What percentage of the members in your church do you think believe the facts about Jesus without committing themselves to that truth?
5. What do you hope to learn from this study?

1

The Foundation of Christian Joy

Philippians 1:1-11

Our study in Philippians is driven by a desire to know the true joy that comes only from Jesus Christ. Before we can adequately pursue joy, however, we must have some kind of an understanding of what it is that we are looking for.

Happiness is situational. We are happy when our team wins; when the girl we love says "yes" to our marriage proposal; when we are given a promotion; when our presentation goes well; when we pick up our brand new vehicle or move into our dream house. These "joys" are temporary (Usually the payments extend well beyond the period of happiness).

These great times may be followed by experiences that plunge us into depression and discouragement. A child rebels against our values, a presentation doesn't go well, we face conflict in the work-place (or church), our health falters, a relationship ends, or unex-pected expenses can hurl us into financial turmoil. All of these circumstances can leave us feeling like we are riding a roller coaster in our life.

The joy the Bible talks about is something that is unaffected by circumstances. It is a state of mind and an orientation of the heart. True joy runs deep. It is a settled state of contentment, confidence and hope. Paul lays a foundation for us in Philippians 1:1-11.

JOY IS BASED IN COMMUNITY
In the opening words following the salutation, Paul writes,
> *I thank my God every time I remember you. In all my prayers for all of you, I always pray with joy because of your partnership in the gospel from the first day until now,. . . . It is right for me to feel this way about all of you, since I have you in my heart; for whether I am in chains or defending and confirming the gospel, all of you share in God's grace with me. God can testify how I long for all of you with the affection of Christ Jesus.* (Philippians 1:3-5, 7-8)

Paul expresses his joy "because of your partnership in the gospel". His joy was not anchored to circumstance but was based in the things he held in common with believers everywhere.

You will not find joy in isolation. If you were stranded on an island someplace you might learn about God's provision. You might come to a deeper relationship with Him, but your joy would be lacking. Joy is fostered in community. It is like saying you can't experience the blessing of marriage unless you have a mate. Joy and others go together.

There are several good reasons for this,
- Other believers are often God's agents of joy. A smile from a Christian friend can turn a bad day into a good day.
- Other believers are our outlet for joy. There is nothing like a shared experience to increase our joy. Think about a great experience you've had like the birth of a child, or a special award, or a great accomplishment. Whatever the event, your joy was made complete as you shared it with others. That same situation in isolation would be rather empty.
- Our Christian family helps us maintain focus. Our fellow

believers notice when we are drifting from the path of joy and point us in the right direction again.

• The Christian community is the laboratory of faith. The Bible is filled with commands that involve "one another". We can't find the joy of obedience if we don't do the laboratory work.

This is why people head to athletic events. Many of these games could be watched on television or listened to on the radio. So why do people go to a game in the heat, cold, rain or snow? It is because of the chance to talk about the last play or to debate strategy with those around you. There is something special about sharing the experience with another.

If you are not involved in a Church home, you need to find one. Find a good church where God's Word is proclaimed and God's people take that Word to heart. God intends for you to be part of a community of faith. Join hands with others for the wonderful journey of joy.

JOY IS ANCHORED TO GOD'S PROMISE

In my experience, Paul's next statement is one of the greatest reasons for joy we have,

> *being confident of this, that he who began a good work in you will carry it on to completion until the day of Christ Jesus.* [Philippians 1:6]

Paul is noted for his deep theology couched in simple statements. In this one verse in Philippians Paul gives us the foundation for joy we need. If you memorize and meditate on just this one verse you will be headed in the direction of joy. Notice the three things Paul affirms in this simple passage.

It was God who began the work of salvation. In other words, God is the one responsible for our salvation. The Bible tells us that even our *faith* is something that God creates in us. (Eph. 2:8,9..." "*For it is by grace you have been saved, through faith and **this not from yourselves**, it is the gift of God, not by works, so that no one can boast.*") The faith is not from us . . .it is a gift of God! Our salvation is not based on our goodness, but on His grace! It is not anchored to how obedient we are (we all fall short here) but in the work that God has done for us and in us. Listen to the words of Jesus in John 6,

> *The Spirit gives life; the flesh counts for nothing...He went on to say, "This is why I told you that no one can come to me unless the Father has enabled him. . . . From this time many of his disciple turned back and no longer followed him.* (John 6:63-66)

These words are difficult to hear because we live in a world that proclaims that the flesh (or what we do) counts for everything. We want to believe that we are masters of our own destiny. And as in the days of Jesus, many hear these words about God's responsibility for our salvation and they turn away. But the Bible is clear, unless God first works in us, we will never come to Him (*"No one can come to me unless the Father who sent me draws him, and I will raise him up at the last day"* John 6:44). God is responsible for our salvation . . . and *only* He is responsible! God gives us faith, His Spirit convicts us of our sin, and His love provided the payment for our sin.

Do you see the practical value of this doctrine? It means that you don't need to DO anything before you can know the forgiveness and life that comes from the Father. You don't have to be a better person; you don't need to know a little more; you don't need to first conquer your addiction, you don't have to get your life in order. You can come to Him NOW. Salvation is not about our goodness but His. It is about what God has done on our behalf.

God continues the work of salvation. We are told that He "began" the work. Salvation is a process. Like in our physical life, we are born spiritual infants and we need time to grow. Christians stumble. Christians make mistakes. We are people "in the process" of salvation.

How quick we are to forget this truth. Often we are joyless because we are frustrated by our failures. We look at our flawed lives and conclude that our salvation didn't "take". We know we should be growing, but we think we should be further along than we are. But our joy is not tied to our success but to the realization that

God does not give up on us. He continues working in our lives. He is committed to us more than we are committed to Him.

A Professor doesn't feel that his or her job is completed because he or she convinced someone to take the class they were teaching. That is just the first step. From that first day of class the good Professor sets out to instruct, inspire, and enrich his or her students. The best Professor will find a way to teach each student. They will provide different kinds of learning experiences. They will tutor students after class. They will patiently respond to e-mails. They will work hard at educating. For the best teachers, it is not about tuition, it is about education.

God is more committed to you than any teacher of the year. When you trust Him, He begins the process of teaching you about life. And He will not quit until He has accomplished His goal. And that leads us to the next point.

God will finish what He started. This is the basis of our confidence, our peace, and our joy. God has promised to finish what He has started in us. We call this the doctrine of the Perseverance of the saints, or the doctrine of Eternal Security. Some people have summarized the doctrine as "once saved, always saved." Our joy comes from this assurance of our salvation. We know joy in life because we *know* where we are headed. The Bible tells us that NOTHING will separate us from Him. (Romans 8:31-39);

Jesus said,

> *I give them eternal life, and they shall **never** perish; **no one** can snatch them out of my hand. My Father, who has given them to me, is greater than all; **no one** can snatch them out of my Father's hand* (John 10:28, 29)

Do you understand what Jesus is telling us? He is saying that once we give our lives to Him He will never let us go. NEVER. We are eternally His. The true believer . . . the person who has really begun to experience the start of God's transformation, is a person who has received a deposit (the Holy Spirit) that **GUARANTEES** our inheritance (Ephesians 1:14).

Can you see how this clear teaching of the Bible serves as a foundation for our joy? If you KNEW that you were headed for heaven, would you be able to relax and enjoy the journey? Of course you would.

Much of Christian teaching today lacks and even dismisses this element of confidence. The focus is on human ability and responsibility. I've heard some use the analogy that the road to heaven is like a highway. God has provided the road but it is up to us whether we get on the road and whether we stay on the road. We can get off at any time. We can get lost, we can become disoriented, and unless we stay on the road we won't get to Heaven. By this teaching we can never really be *sure* that we are going to Heaven.

Here's what happens in the life of the one who has no assurance of salvation. Instead of living joyfully we are tentative. We enjoy our salvation now but we are uncertain if it will last. We are always looking over our shoulder. We are justifiably concerned that we are going to make that fatal mistake that will void our reservation in Heaven. So we spend our life focused on our behavior and effort rather than resting in His grace. Our "joy" comes and goes depending on how well we are performing.

I respectfully disagree with my brothers and sisters who hold to the aforementioned opinion. I just don't think it is consistent with what the Bible teaches. Even the most famous verse in the Bible seems to speak of being sure of salvation, *"For God so loved the world that he gave his only begotten Son, so that whosoever believeth in him would not perish but have everlasting life."* (John 3:16). We are told that those who believe **have** everlasting life. Let me ask a simple question. If you have *everlasting* life, can you lose it?

For some reason, when presented with the doctrine of eternal security some people bristle. They say the notion of God being responsible for our salvation "violates our freedom!" But these people are looking at it the wrong way. Let me try to illustrate the concept.

Suppose you were in the middle of a big lake. You become sick and you can no longer swim. The lifeguard swims out to you and grabs you. He begins the process of bringing you back to shore. Sensing your anxiety he says to you, "don't worry, I won't let you go". Do you complain that your freedom has been violated? Do you fight him because He is diminishing you as a person? No, you know you are helpless. You cannot make it on your own. The only hope you have is for the lifeguard to take hold of you . . . and never let you go. You welcome his firm grip. And as the lifeguard swims closer and closer to the shore you begin to relax and feel more and more confident. With every stroke you believe that the lifeguard is true to his word . . . He will bring you home. He will not let you go.

It is the same with our salvation. We are not offended by God's promise because we know that without it, we will inevitably drift away. We are helpless without Him. If my salvation depended on my ability to stay the course, I would inevitably turn the wrong direction.

But that leads to a second objection; "eternal security leads to passive faith". It is argued that if we know that our salvation is guaranteed, we will stop working. But once again this shows a misunderstanding of God's salvation. Salvation is a process. God has given us His Spirit to cultivate our hearts and develop a Christlike spirit within us. God's commitment to us does not end when we "say a prayer". His desire is for us to be "conformed to the image of His son" (Romans 8:29)

Can we resist this work? Sure we can. There are people who seem to fall away from the faith all the time. But have these people *lost* their salvation or did they never really have it to start with?

One of the weaknesses of the church today is our emphasis on "having an experience". We play soft music and urge people to walk forward, raise their hand, and say a prayer. If they respond to the stimuli then we pronounce them "born again". Unfortunately many of these folks have *not* been truly re-born, they have just had a nice experience. They have not really counted the cost or understood the nature of the commitment they were making.

I believe people "fall away from the faith" because they act without knowledge. They respond to the gospel in the same way they impulsively order a product from an infomercial. They are moved by the sales pitch but have not thought through what they were doing.

This is why it is so important that we take care in our evangelism. We must work to make sure a person knows what "being a Christian" means before we push them to "respond". We must seek to make disciples rather than merely get "decisions". Those who are truly born again can be certain that He who began that work in them will finish that work.

Can you be a true believer and still resist God's work in their life? Of course you can. In fact, we all resist His work at times. And when this happens God must break our will. Let's go back to the lifeguard analogy. If you fight the lifeguard, he will either take a stronger hold (and it may hurt), he may pull you under water (so you stop fighting. . . He or she knows they can hold their breath longer than you can) or they may eventually draw away from you. The lifeguard will let you wear yourself out. But he will not let you drown. When you are ready to stop fighting him, He will bring you back to safety. You will be miserable as long as you resist.

So it is with the believer. We can fight God. We can resist His work in our life but it is foolish to do so. God will allow us to kick and scream. He will let us fight and wear ourselves out by our foolishness. But eventually, when we tire, He will continue His work. He will not let us drown. He may have to use strong tactics to save us . . . but He *will* save us.

Do you see why this is such an important issue? Do you see how joy comes from trusting God's promise? No matter how foolish we are, God will not abandon us. No matter how bad the circumstances of life may become we know that He is going to finish His work in our life. We may be fickle, but God is not. We may stumble but He will help us up. This one promise in Philippians 1:6 will make a tremendous difference in our outlook on life. The doctrine of eternal security means,
- we can be bold rather than tentative
- we can be confident rather than nervous
- we can be grateful rather than uncertain
- we can rejoice rather than be afraid
- we can proclaim with confidence (and without arrogance) that we are sure we are headed to Heaven.

JOY INCREASES OVER TIME

And this is my prayer: that your love may abound

*more and more in knowledge and depth of insight,
so that you may be able to discern what is best and
may be pure and blameless until the day of Christ,
filled with the fruit of righteousness that comes
through Jesus Christ—to the glory and praise of
God.* [Phil. 1:9-11]

Paul prayed for the continued growth of the believers in Philippi. Joy increases as we grow in the faith. The Christian life is not static . . . it is growing. Our joy increases as we see ourselves becoming more and more like Christ.

Can you see why some believers lack joy? Many begin their Christian life in a cloud of joy but that cloud gradually dissipates. By the time they have been a "believer" for a couple of years they are often just "going through the motions". Faith is lifeless. These people (real or superficial believers) have stopped growing. Their faith has atrophied.

Paul urges us to remember that salvation is a process. I AM saved because of Christ has paid for my sin. I AM BEING saved as God's Spirit transforms me. I WILL BE SAVED on that day when I escape this earthly body and am purified of the old man.

Several years ago when we were on vacation we went white water rafting. At first we got into the water and enjoyed maneuvering the boat in the gentle current. As we drifted down river we faced a couple of "little rapids" and really enjoyed them. At this point I thought, "This is a piece of cake!"

As the journey continued we faced some fierce rapids. We had to work hard and work together to maneuver through those areas of the river. At times it was quite harrowing. But the enjoyment from the fierce rapids was superior to the enjoyment from the little rapids. We would have missed out on the real joy of white water rafting if we had gotten out of the water after the first set of rapids.

The Christian life is like that. We miss out if we stop progressing. The initial stages of the faith are enjoyable but they are nothing compared with what God will introduce us to as we continue to travel with Him. We must keep paddling.

The work of God in us is like the work of building a house. At times you see great progress (like when a carpenter is putting up the frame of the structure). These are exciting times. But there are other times when progress seems slow or non-existent (such as when you are sanding, staining, doing the wiring and "mudding" drywall). But all of these things are part of the finished product. You need both the frame and the detail to produce a home you can enjoy.

The same is true of the Christian life. There are times when you will see rapid growth and dramatic change. Thank God for those times. At other times you may feel that God has stopped working in your life. But that will never happen . . . He may just be doing some finish work on some areas of your character before He begins in another area of your life. It could be that you are fighting Him in the process by your reckless living (akin to bad weather to the builder). But He has not abandoned His work . . . He will continue it until that great and glorious day when He calls us home to Himself.

PRACTICALLY SPEAKING

How do we keep from hindering the building process? Let me give you some suggestions,

- Commit Philippians 1:6 to memory. Don't just memorize the words; take them to heart. Make them the foundation on which you build your life and anchor your joy. Consider the fabulous implications of this great promise of God. When you begin to feel you don't have enough strength to carry on remember that it is not your strength or your faith that saves you but His mercy and grace.
- Get a sign (don't steal it) that says, "Construction Zone" and place it on the door of your office or room as a reminder that God is at Work in your life.
- Meet regularly with some Christian friends to talk about your spiritual life. Share the joy of what God is doing in your lives. Begin your conversation with a simple question, "What have you learned about God or experienced from God that has helped you look past the circumstances of life and focus on the greatness of your relationship with Him?"
- Regularly do a spiritual inventory of your life to monitor your growth. Are you increasing in joy or beginning to drift? Is

your worship more honest or is it becoming superficial? Are you making progress in the troublesome areas of your life (anxiety, temper, gossip and so forth)? This regular inventory will help keep you on track.

We are part of a tremendous movement of God. Our experience of joy is firmly anchored in God's work and promise. We can live with confidence of our eternal destiny not because of our goodness but because of His. We proclaim we are going to Heaven not out of arrogance (unless you think you are going there because you are better than most people) but because of God's promise.

There are no gimmicks or programs we need to master in order to experience God's joy. If we have truly responded to the invitation of God's grace, then the Spirit of joy already lives in us. God has given us the Spirit as a "deposit that guarantees our inheritance". Our task is to learn to trust that same Spirit to do His work in us and through us.

Study Questions
1. How is the shared joy of Christianity different from the joy of the world? How is it the same?
2. What does Philippians 1:6 mean to you? What difference would it make to you practically if you *really* believed this promise that God, who began the work in you, is also going to see that work to completion?
3. How does your church view the issue of the doctrine known as eternal security? What objections do you still have to this doctrine? Try to state the author's position clearly and fairly.
4. How does the lifeguard illustration help you understand the doctrine more clearly?
5. Do you agree with author's contention that joy should increase as we progress in the Christian faith? Why or why not?

2

Finding Joy in the Difficult Times

Philippians 1:12-18

A n oxymoron is the joining of two words that don't seem to go together. For example: light darkness, a deafening silence, a bold retreat, a powerful servant, a short sermon . . . . you get the idea. And any time someone begins to talk about being joyful in trials it sounds like an oxymoron. We think of joy as being something that takes place in pleasant times. Joy accompanies good times, not difficult times.

And this is part of our problem. We have a narrow view of joy. We think of joy as that illusive feeling while everything is running smoothly and we are able to have everything we want. We look around and think the joyful people are the ones who have everything.

The apostle Paul however, advertises a joy that is deeper than anything we have conceived with our minds. It is a joy independent of circumstances. It is present in the delightful and good times . . . but it is also present in the difficult and painful times.

JOY IN DIFFICULT CIRCUMSTANCES

Paul was in jail in Rome. He was there after being framed for a crime he didn't commit. He had been in jail for well over two years (he spent two years in Caesarea and then appealed his case to Rome). Everybody knew about Paul's arrest and the Philippians had written to find out how he was "holding up".

It is hard to imagine what it was like to be in Paul's situation. He was isolated from friends and family. They could visit but many surely stayed away. The same thing happens when someone goes to jail or prison in our time. If you are convicted of a crime some people will immediately disassociate from you. They don't want to be tainted by your "reputation". They may not even take the time to find out the circumstances of your situation. They forget that everyone does dumb and sinful things on occasion.

The time in prison is very lonely. A person sentenced to prison is often hours from family and friends. They may go weeks without a visit from a friendly face. Each day they look forward to mail delivery and often their spirits are crushed with disappointment. I suspect Paul faced the same thing. Some of his friends remained loyal. Others seemed to forget him. It must have been a lonely time.

He was unable to do what he loved doing. Paul was called to the gospel ministry. He loved proclaiming God's Word. For over two years he had been kept from preaching in the synagogue and prohibited from teaching in the churches. He was unable to debate the learned men of the city. This was Paul's passion . . . it was where he really seemed to "shine". Paul couldn't do what he enjoyed most. It would be like a musician who couldn't sing or couldn't play their instrument. It was like an artist who could no longer paint. It was a frustrating time.

Paul had lost any sense of personal freedom. He was chained to a Roman guard by a short chain on his wrist at all times. He had absolutely no privacy. The guard witnessed even the most private acts and heard every private word. It must have been demeaning and dehumanizing!

Paul had many of these struggles in his life. In the book of 2 Corinthians Paul tells us some of his story,

I have been in prison more frequently, been flogged more severely, and been exposed to death again and again. Five times I received from the Jews the forty lashes minus one. Three times I was beaten with rods, once I was stoned, three times I was ship-wrecked, I spent a night and a day in the open sea, I have been constantly on the move. I have been in danger from rivers, in danger from bandits, in danger from my own countrymen, in danger from Gentiles; in danger in the city, in danger in the country, in danger at sea; and in danger from false brothers. I have labored and toiled and have often gone without sleep; I have known hunger and thirst and have often gone without food; I have been cold and naked. [2 Corinthians 11:23-29]

I bet it was tough for Paul to get insurance! It would also be tough for Paul to remain positive and joyful. But in spite of all that had happened, Paul was joyful.

Don't miss an important point here. Paul is a bold example that things do not always go well with followers of Christ. Sometimes circumstances *are* difficult. These difficult times come even to those who are living faithful lives. This is important to hear because sometimes we believe (and sometimes are taught) that godly people are spared difficult times. We seem to think that when hard things come into our lives, God is punishing us for something. But that is not necessarily true!

Things may be going well for you. Perhaps you are healthy, wealthy, popular, and things are running smoothly. If so, I applaud your good fortune. But please don't conclude that your blessings mean that God approves of you more than others. That reasoning does not hold up under scrutiny. If it did, then it would mean that Paul and the rest of the apostles (who were all persecuted) were not as spiritually advanced as you.

On the other hand, it may be important that you see that the chains you wear do not mean God has turned away from you. Your chain may be a devastating illness, financial stress, emotional struggles, or relationship problems. You may feel you are walking under a perpetual dark cloud . . . you are in good company. Faithful people sometimes are asked to endure the chains of life.

With that said, listen to what Paul writes to the Philippians as he faces his difficult circumstances.

> *Now I want you to know, brothers, that what has happened to me has really served to advance the gospel. As a result, it has become clear throughout the whole palace guard and to everyone else that I am in chains for Christ. Because of my chains, most of the brothers in the Lord have been encouraged to speak the word of God more courageously and fearlessly. [Phil. 1:12-14]*

Paul could have grumbled. He could have pled his case. He could have been bitter, or discouraged. But he wasn't! Instead, Paul declared that God was using his circumstances. He pointed to two immediate positive results from his circumstances.

First, the Imperial guard had heard the Gospel. The Imperial Guard was a group of elite soldiers, stationed in Rome. They were there primarily to protect the Emperor. At times there were between 10,000 and 16,000 of these troops stationed in Rome. Apparently these men also served as guards over the prisoners in Rome.

Paul was bound to one of these men with a short length of chain on his wrist. Every four hours the guard would change. I'm sure some of the guards were harsh and some were friendly. All of them were too close! Yet, instead of being bitter about this invasion of his personal "space" Paul saw an opportunity. He realized that he was not only chained to soldiers . . . they were chained to him!

Paul had a "captive audience". For four hours at a time Paul could talk to these men about Jesus Christ. Six different men each day! What a challenge! What an opportunity! Apparently, his witness was effective. Paul remarks that because of his imprisonment, the gospel of Jesus Christ was known throughout the whole Praetorian Guard. I would bet that each day the guards would draw straws to see who would have to be chained to Paul. It is assumed (since he sends greetings from those in Caesar's household, Phil.

4:22) that the gospel message had even worked its way into the Emperor's home. Apparently some of the guards listened, believed, and shared with others.

There was also a second benefit to his situation. Paul tells us that as a result of his imprisonment others spoke the word of Christ more courageously and fearlessly. God used Paul's situation to "light a fire" under some of the other believers. Perhaps they were encouraged to carry on Paul's work while he was unable to do the work himself. Maybe these people were inspired by Paul's example. Whatever the reason, the message was being proclaimed more boldly because of Paul's situation. We see this happen when,

- A church crisis brings the people together
- A Pastoral vacancy motivates leaders into action
- A person contracts a disease and their positive attitude towards their sickness spurs others on in their own faithfulness.
- A church faces persecution in a communist country. Often when the curtain of persecution is lifted, we find a church that is strong and growing. The Christian people had to make a choice; they couldn't sit on the fence. Their faith became precious.
- A Christian is jailed for refusal to compromise and others are encouraged to be more committed.

Now I realize that it may not be as easy for you to see anything positive in your circumstances. In fact, you may even bristle at the idea that anyone would suggest that something positive could come from the devastating circumstances of your present situation. But please don't give up on me. I think there are at least a couple of principles in Paul's story to help us find joy even in the most difficult circumstances of life.

First, we learn that **though we cannot control our circumstances, we can control our response to them.** We don't have to despair when tough times come. We don't have to withdraw. These are choices we make. Paul reminds us that whether a difficult circumstance defeats us or deepens us depends on how we respond to it.

It is natural to feel sorry for yourself. (I happen to be very good at feeling sorry for myself). It is natural for us to wonder, "Why me?" But Paul shows us that we can CHOOSE to be joyful. We can choose to trust the Sovereign hand of God even when we don't see clearly. We can choose to believe that God is indeed working for the good . . . even though the evidence seems illusive. It won't remove the pain . . . but it will enable us to live joyfully in spite of it. We must decide to focus on the wisdom and strength of the Problem Solver rather than on the problem.

Second, **we need to look for opportunities rather than wallow in our liabilities.** Paul saw an opportunity to share with those he would not encounter any other way. He used his chains as a teaching tool that could strengthen others. He chose to dig deeper rather than to be swept away. Let me give you some examples,

- You can grumble about being homebound or you can take that time to do the reading, writing and praying you've always said you wished you had time to do.
- You can grumble about financial stresses or you can take them as a challenge to find contentment and joy in things that don't cost money.
- You can grumble about your physical condition or use your physical condition as your motivation for getting started on that exercise program you've been putting off.
- You can complain about how empty the house is with the kids gone or you can travel and develop new hobbies and interests.
- You can grumble about your illness or you can use the time to deepen your faith and to minister to the medical personnel and other patients you will find in waiting rooms
- You can complain about where you live, or draw from the benefits of the place where God has planted you.
- You can grumble about your income or you can have fun and be creative as you try to see how much you can do with a limited income.

Think about the many people we encounter in the difficult times who we may not see any other time: doctors, nurses, technicians, judges, police officers, social workers, and troubled people of many types. There are other students, neighbors, friends, who have had similar sorrows. If we would stop feeling sorry for ourselves and look around for opportunities to glorify God . . . . we would be astounded at the opportunities available to us. We would find unexpected joy as we used those opportunities for God's glory.

JOY WHEN DEALING WITH DIFFICULT PEOPLE

Dealing with difficult circumstances is one thing but dealing with difficult people is another. Paul not only faced the problem of his imprisonment, he also had to endure attacks from other Christians. In the military we would say he was being threatened by "friendly fire". These were fellow believers . . . or at least they professed to be. Paul says, they were "preaching Christ." They were not false teachers, they were teaching truth but with a contentious spirit. Listen to how Paul describes the situation,

> *It is true that some preach Christ out of envy and rivalry, but others out of goodwill. The latter do so in love, knowing that I am put here for the defense of the gospel. The former preach Christ out of selfish ambition, not sincerely, supposing that they can stir up trouble for me while I am in chains. But what does it matter? The important thing is that in every way, whether from false motives or true, Christ is preached. And because of this I rejoice.* (1:15-18)

Have you been in this kind of situation? Perhaps in a time of need some person decided to take that opportunity to point out everything you've ever done wrong in your life. Maybe you have encountered a fellow employee who used your illness to try to steal your job. Perhaps you faced a family crisis and found rejection rather than love from other believers. Maybe you made a difficult decision and others attacked your character. Maybe your church was going through a difficult time and another congregation saw this as an opportunity to steal your flock.

Paul tells us that the people attacking him were preaching out of "selfish ambition, not sincerely, seeking to stir up trouble for him." They were not motivated by a desire to reach others for Christ . . . their motive was to attack the competition! In some way, they saw

Paul's imprisonment as a chance for them to get ahead. They saw their service to Christ as some kind of competition.

The Joyful Response to Difficult People

Paul told Titus that he should warn a divisive person once, and then have nothing more to do with them. In this letter, Paul pleads with two women in the church to agree with each other. Paul told the church in Corinth that cliques were stupid and destructive. He confronted false teachers and he even stood up to Peter and told him he was being inconsistent. And to be honest, I would have expected Paul to come after these difficult people with great energy. But he doesn't. Instead he says simply, "*What does it matter? The important thing is that in every way, whether from false motives or true, Christ is preached. And because of this I rejoice.*"

What are we to make of this? When should we confront difficult people and when should we back off? When do we fight and when should we shrug? Here's what I see in Paul's example: Paul was fierce when the gospel was perverted; he was fierce when the unity of the church was threatened; but he was passive when the attacks were personal.

Do you notice that his approach is the opposite of the way we handle things. We are immediately aroused to anger when personally attacked and often unmoved when the gospel is distorted and we want to "stay out of it" when the unity of the church is at stake. Many of the times when we feel we are fierce in "defending the faith", we are really just seeking to defend ourselves.

Paul understood that HE was not the issue. Did he want to be liked? I'm sure he did. Did it hurt when these men sought to use his problems for their advantage . . . you bet. But Paul overlooked the personal affront and celebrated the fact that God's word was being proclaimed.

Paul knew these men would have to give an account for their methods and motives. But that wasn't his job. God has told us not to retaliate. He has told us to leave judgment to Him. He has told us to love our enemies. And when we do what God says we will have joy.

When you think about it, Paul's counsel makes a great deal of sense practically.

1. Difficult people are diffused more quickly when we don't fight them. They love the battle and it's no fun when we won't engage them. Maybe that was what Paul meant when he told Titus to warn a divisive person once and then stop fighting them. To go over an issue again and again only makes more of an issue of it. If you don't "let it go" the problem takes on a life of it's own.
2. We should remember that the worst thing anyone says about us is still not even close to what COULD be said about us. If people knew me like I know me . . . they could say so much more!
3. Our true joy is not anchored to the opinion of the crowd. True, deep, and lasting joy is concerned about the opinion of the Lord.
4. When we seek to love rather than strike back we often find that our enemies become our friends.

Practically Speaking

Let me give you three final principles we learn about dealing with difficult people. First, **we learn that we must always look at the big picture.** We are seeking to build the Kingdom of God . . .not a kingdom to ourselves. What people say about us is so much less important than what they say about the Lord. We should be willing for God to use us in any way He deems appropriate if it will get the message out. . . .even if this is at the cost of our own reputation. Our joy must be anchored in His glory . . . not ours.

Second, we must remember that **we have done foolish and sinful things**. I don't think Paul ever forgot that at one time he was zealous but wrong. At one time he persecuted Christians. He had them executed. He meant well. He thought he was serving the Lord. But what he was doing was wrong. Sometimes well meaning people do hurtful things and don't realize what they are doing. We must continue to act with grace, even when others do not act that way toward us. Someday we may need that same grace.

Finally, **we must remember that even though other people will disappoint us, God will not.** If we anchor our joy to the behavior of others, we will ride a roller coaster all our life. People are inconsistent. And it is not just other people. We want to live godly lives, but sometimes we look more like the Devil than we do the Lord. Our job is to remember that our confidence does not rest in our ability, but His. If we will focus on Christ we will be able to endure any crisis.

You see this in the lives of martyrs again and again. They were taken to a cross to be burned and died singing in the flames. They were thrown to the lions and died refusing to renounce their faith and testifying of the Lord's greatness. These great saints blessed those who ridiculed them. They extended love even as they received hatred. They rejoiced even as their body was devastated by disease or persecution. They were able to do these things because they trusted God rather than men or the circumstances of life.

The best example of all was a man who spent His life trying to help others. In return He was despised and rejected. He spoke of love and was tortured and executed. He extended forgiveness to His attackers . . . even as He was nailed to a cross.

People will disappoint us . . . but God never will. He proved it at Calvary and if you give Him a chance He will prove it in your life. If we remember this; if we trust God rather than others; we will discover that joy in difficult times is not an oxymoron, it is a reality we can celebrate.

Study Questions
1. What has been the most difficult time of your life? As you look back can you see anything that God was doing through this painful circumstance?
2. In your experience what is the more difficult trial: painful circumstances or difficult people?
3. Have you ever tried to CHOOSE your attitude? What happened? Why must we take responsibility for the way we respond to circumstances?
4. Why is it helpful when dealing with difficult people to remember the times when we were the difficult people? What perspective does it give us toward our antagonist?
5. Why are we so prone to tie our joy to our circumstances?

3

Living Joyfully in Life and in Death

Philippians 1:19-26

As a Pastor, I've been called into a number of heartbreaking circumstances. I've officiated at funerals of children (always a devastating circumstance), of murder victims, of those who suffered from AIDS, and those who committed suicide. I have waited in hospital rooms or homes for the inevitable last breath of one who has suffered long. I've visited with those headed to prison and counseled those who were devastated by a relationship they could not save. Sometimes life stinks.

These are the situations that make us wonder if it is really possible to have joy in *every* circumstance? How can you rejoice when life is caving in around you? How do you rejoice as you stand eyeball to eyeball with death? Perhaps as you read this you are a person who

- Has been diagnosed with a terminal illness and face an uncertain result from disease treatment
- Has a body that is getting some age on it. Your blood pressure is high, you can't tell the difference between indigestion and

chest pains, and you aren't sure whether you have taken your medicine or haven't done so.

- Is facing a serious surgery. You've signed the papers. You know the risks. You've heard the stories of people who go into surgery and never come out.
- Is left behind after someone you love has died. The ache of loneliness is ever-present. Your friends were supportive for a while but now they have moved on with their lives and your pain continues with no one to help you bear it.
- Has been encouraged to take early retirement (or be terminated) even though you aren't ready to be retired.
- Has had to watch your children move to another part of the world with the grandchildren you long to know.

If this list describes you, you may be wondering how you are supposed to rejoice in your situation. I bet it was a struggle for you to even begin reading this chapter. You don't want to hear more empty platitudes or trite catch phrases. You're tired of people who don't understand telling you to "have faith".

I don't plan to speak as one who understands. I honestly don't understand. All I know for sure is that your pain is deeper than I can comprehend. But Paul does understand. In Philippians 1:19-26 we find a record of Paul wrestling with the temporary nature of his own life. He knew that at any moment the fickle Nero might decide to cut off his head. He knew that he might be in his jail cell for the rest of his life. (I wonder which possibility scared him the most.) He knew he might never see his dearest friends again on this side of the grave. Paul understood what you are going through. And he has something to teach you and something to teach me. Read his words slowly and carefully,

> *I know that through your prayers and the help given by the Spirit of Jesus Christ, what has happened to me will turn out for my deliverance. I eagerly expect and hope that I will in no way be ashamed, but will have sufficient courage so that now as always, Christ will be exalted in my body, whether by life or*

by death. For to me, to live is Christ and to die is gain. If I am to go on living in the body, this will mean fruitful labor for me. Yet what shall I choose? I do not know! I am torn between the two: I desire to depart and be with Christ, which is better by far; but it is more necessary for you that I remain in the body. Convinced of this, I know that I will remain, and I will continue with all of you for your progress and joy in the faith, so that through my being with you again your joy in Christ Jesus will overflow on account of me. (Philippians 1:19-26)

Paul Viewed Death With a Joyful Perspective

Before we can understand how Paul could maintain his joy in such difficult times of life, we must understand Paul's view of death. How a person views death is the key to how well they will enjoy life. The wrong view of death leaves us fearful with an increasing sense of futility. We become paralyzed by the dark shadow that may lurk around the next corner. But we must face this shadow of death if we are ever going to be free to live.

Paul Viewed Death not as Loss but as Gain

As Paul sat in his jail cell, he knew that at any moment his life could be snatched from him. He knew he was innocent, but he also knew Nero. Nero was well known for his arbitrary executions. But Paul did not despair. He didn't withdraw or become filled with fear and apprehension. In fact, Paul seemed unconcerned about death.

In the mind of Paul death was "gain" rather than loss. The only people we know who talk like this are those who are suffering and long for death to end that suffering. We don't hear this kind of attitude around the water cooler at work. We are much more likely to talk about people "losing the battle" with their disease. When someone we love dies we often say we have "lost them." When treatments are exhausted Doctors say, "There is nothing more we can do" in an attitude of defeat and resignation. We usually view death as the ultimate defeat. But that is not Paul's attitude. He viewed death as the ultimate victory.

Paul wrote about his desire to "depart" to be with Christ. The word translated "depart" is the same word for "striking camp". In other words, it is the idea of taking your tent down and moving on. This word is also used to describe pulling up the anchor of a ship. Both images reveal the temporary nature of the present condition.

In 2 Corinthians 5 we read these familiar words from Paul

Now we know that if the earthly tent we live in is destroyed, we have a building from God, an eternal house in heaven, not built by human hands. (2 Corinthians 5:1)

Paul taught that life is just the first stop in the journey of existence. Death is the transfer point that leads us to home. When I went to High School in Chicago I used to take a bus from the school to the subway. The subway would take me most of the way home but I still had to get off the subway and onto another bus before I reached my destination. Every time I changed vehicles it was a transfer point. I had to make the transfers in order to get to my destination.

Life is like that. When we are born it is a transfer point. When our body begins to decay, it is a transfer point. When we die, it is a transfer point. None of these points is our true destination . . . they are just parts of the journey. Paul understood that this life is just one leg of our journey. For some, it is a lengthy "ride"; for others, the journey is short. Either way, this life is not the final destination. We all have the same final transfer point and that transfer point is called death.

To Paul, death was not an enemy. To Paul, death was when we finally arrived home. He saw life as something we endured in order to get to Heaven. Death was like a graduation day. Paul focused on the glory that came after death,

- In Heaven we will be free from our nagging sins and limitations
- We will be free from all doubts
- We will have all our questions answered
- We will be free of the Devil's attacks
- We will be set free from our suffering and limitations

- We will understand what God was doing through our life in those hard times
- We will be reunited with friends and family who have gone before us in Christ
- We will see Jesus face to face

When we are able to see what lies beyond death, it takes the fear out of the grave. We may still dread the process of dying (the unknown is always a little scary). . . but we need not fear death itself.

Paul Saw Death as the Blessing of Being With Jesus

Paul told us that he longed to "depart and be with Christ". It was not that Paul didn't want to be with his fellow believers on earth . . . he loved them. It was not that Paul didn't want to be with family and friends. He loved them as well. But IF HE HAD TO CHOOSE, Paul looked forward to getting acquainted with the one who had given His life for Him. He looked forward to meeting the one who had so changed his life.

I have looked forward to meeting authors that have meant much to me. As I approached them the first time, my heart raced and my mind became as Jello. (Why is it that at those times when we want to sound most articulate, suave and intelligent, we almost always end up sounding like an incoherent baboon?) As embarrassing as these occasions sometimes were, those meetings are some of the best memories of my life.

I remember the night I proposed to my wife. I had flowers, a nifty little poem, and I had practiced what I wanted to say. I left my office and headed for home. Wouldn't you know that this night I met the slow freight train . . . which was immediately followed by another freight train going the other way on the tracks! I didn't notice the other drivers in the cars around me. I didn't count the cars in the train. I had one thing on my mind. I wanted to get home to see the woman I loved. I wanted to tell her how much I cared. (For those who care, she was leaving the parking lot as I was pulling in . . . but she came back and said "yes").

If we get this excited to meet those who have influenced us on earth . . . would we not . . . should we not . . . be even more eager to meet the one who has snatched us from the jaws of destruction?

Aren't we eager to meet the one who has loved us from before we were born? This was the kind of anticipation Paul felt as he considered death. He didn't focus on the separation; He focused on Jesus.

Paul saw death as an immediate entrance into God's presence

It is important, I think, to point out one more fact. There is a theological debate as to what happens when we die. Some have said that we will "sleep" until the time of resurrection. I do not believe this is what Jesus or Paul taught. Do you remember when Jesus talked to the thief on the cross? After the thief asked the Savior to "Remember me", Jesus told him," TODAY, you will be with me in paradise." He did not say, "Some day you will be with me" . . . He said, "TODAY." I believe that when a believer dies, he goes immediately into the presence of the Lord.

This passage in Philippians makes the case with emphasis. Understand that Paul is debating which scenario would be better, to die and be with Jesus, or to live on and continue to minister in his name. Do you see that this would be a mute point if we didn't go right into the presence of the Lord at death? What benefit would there be to dying if Paul wasn't going to be with Christ until the second coming? Why not live as long as you can since you aren't going to get home to Heaven any sooner?

Death leads us to Jesus. Death means we go home to Heaven. Death means we are reunited with those who have gone before us. And if we understand the true nature of death, it is difficult to feel sorrow for any believer who dies. We will feel sorrow for our own loss . . . but we should celebrate the good fortune of the one we love.

Practical Lessons About Death

Let's put this all together and draw out some practical lessons. *First, we must expand our view of what "life" really is.* We must constantly remind ourselves that this life is but the prelude to the life that is to come. We need to remember that "this world is not my home . . . I'm only passing through."

The gospel message is not designed PRIMARILY to help us in this life. It certainly does help in the here and now but that is not the primary purpose. The primary message of the gospel is that through

Christ we can know glorious life beyond the grave. This life is just the title page of the book called life. The real story is yet to come.

Second, *we must deliberately focus on the benefits of Heaven rather than the pain of loss.* I've sent one child to college and another will be heading off to college soon. My children and I see this experience differently. They look forward to the challenge, the freedom, the new beginning and the new friends. They are eager to get on with their lives and to begin making a significant contribution to the world. They are eager to make their own way and to start their own families. This is a wonderfully exciting time (even though it is a little scary). My attitude is different. I see loss. I feel like I am losing one who has been such an important and treasured part of my life. I know that my relationship with my child will never again be the same. I see separation and emptiness.

When it comes to death, we have a choice. We can look at death and Heaven like the student or like the parent. We can see possibilities or we mourn change. As we go through life we can focus on the process or the destination. We can get discouraged by the obstacles or become more determined to reach our destination in spite of the obstacles. Our focus is the key to our view of death. What about you? Do you see death as the end or as a transfer point? One view leads to despair, the other leads to hope.

The Right Perspective on Life

I know what you're thinking. Some of you would much prefer death to the pain and agony of the present. You aren't looking for information on Heaven, you want help for the present. Hang with me. Once we understand death it becomes much easier to face the difficult circumstances of life. Tim Stafford gives a very helpful illustration of what you and I need to understand.

> Pain and sorrow are transformed by the view from the end. If we walk through a hospital, we can encounter a practical example of this. There is one particular ward where moans are most likely to assault our ears. Young women writhe in severe and helpless pain. Their problem is obvious to the eye: their stomachs have swelled to the size of beach

balls. The taut skin glistens. As the hours pass, the women's faces grow increasingly worn with pain. If they were there with any other diagnosis, say cancer, the scene would cut our hearts.

Instead, we feel great joy in a maternity ward. The women there may be feeling as much pain as women with stomach cancer, but they look confidently toward a different end — a joyful end. Later, they will not even remember much of the process. How often have we heard a mother say, "Isn't it strange how you can't remember how much it hurt?" The pain that seemed so terrible has faded away because it came to its proper end: she holds her baby.[1]

Isn't that a great picture? Life is sometimes painful but we endure it because we know what is on the other side of the pain. Like many women reaching the point of delivery we may face anxiety as we approach the day of death. We may want to say, "No, I've changed my mind, I don't want to do it!" But we know that is no longer an option. Once we are born we know we will face death. When the time of "labor" comes, we must keep our eyes on the goal. We get through the times of pain by keeping perspective. We must constantly look beyond the pain and see where we are headed.

Paul proclaimed confidence that he was going to survive his present crisis because he felt his work was not yet done. He expressed his gratitude for the prayers of the Philippians and the strength of God's Spirit. He believed the prayers of the Philippians would help him get through the present crisis.

I know that through your prayers and the help given
by the Spirit of Jesus Christ, what has happened to
me will turn out for my deliverance. (1:19)

Paul never said that the difficult times were easy to endure. They weren't. Paul needed support. He craved the prayers of the people. He knew that without God's strength the trials of life could unravel him. Paul leaned on the strength provided him. He *chose* to focus on the blessing rather than the burden. He *chose* to rejoice in the promise rather than despair at the problem.

Sometimes we have the feeling that anyone who admits weakness, anyone who admits that they need help, is spiritually deficient. That's not true. We all need help on occasion. Paul needed the prayers (and even some financial support) of the Philippians. He was encouraged by their visits. Their prayers strengthened him. Ask your friends to hold the rope of your life by their prayers.

Paul's Goal was to Live for Christ

Paul's outlook on life was anchored to his view of death. He makes his grand declaration in verse 21. it is a verse well worth memorizing.

> *For to me, to live is Christ and to die is gain.*

The Living Bible puts this real well, "For to me, living means opportunities for Christ, and dying — well, that's better yet!" Paul saw life as having one primary purpose: "to honor, glorify, enjoy, and build a relationship with Christ." These verses raise the inevitable question, 'What does "living" mean to you?" If you were to fill in the blank: "to me, to live is _____ ." What would you put in the blank? What does "living" mean to you?

Paul was determined to live productively as long as He lived

> *If I am to go on living in the body, this will mean fruitful labor for me. Yet what shall I choose?. . . . I know that I will remain, and I will continue with all of you for your progress and joy in the faith, so that through my being with you again your joy in Christ Jesus will overflow on account of me.*

I admire Paul's attitude. He is determined that if he God grants him continued days on earth he is going to live as productively as possible. Too many of us stop living before we die. Difficult times come and we lie down and prepare to die!

The Bible says nothing about retirement. We may retire from employment . . .but we do not retire from our service to the Lord.

We must honor Him in all our ways for all our days. The Christian life is a marathon, not a sprint. We must not waste the time God gives on earth. Perhaps you can't serve him like you used to serve. Maybe you are living with some restrictions. Don't give up . . work to find new ways to serve!

- Volunteer to cook meals
- Transport people in need
- Write letters to encourage others
- Use the phone to minister to those who suffer
- Pray, pray, pray
- Put your faith story in writing
- Help with projects at the church
- Give financially to support a ministry
- Deepen your faith by reading
- Take time to visit with friends and look for an opportunity to share the gospel message
- Volunteer to answer phones and greet people at the church or for some other ministry
- Tutor a student who is having difficulty
- Help support a single parent, financially, or by helping with childcare

I hope you get the idea . . . you don't have to stop serving the Lord simply because your body can no longer work the same way it used to work. Just because one way of service is closed, we shouldn't give up. Paul was sure of one thing . . . if he was going to live, he was going to seek to be engaged in fruitful labor. This was his attitude whether he was in jail or on the road, whether he was applauded or despised, healthy or sick, had money or didn't have anything.

And this needs to be our attitude as well. It should be our attitude whether we have a disease or are healthy; whether we live in a nursing home or in our own home; whether our memory is sharp, or fuzzy. It doesn't matter . . . as long as we live we should seek to live fruitfully. Our goal should be to honor our great Lord in all our living . . . right up to the last breath of our life.

In 2 Timothy we can read Paul's last recorded words. He's in jail again, and this time Paul knows that the end has arrived. His life is going to end soon. He feels alone. And this is what Paul writes,

For I am already being poured out like a drink offering, and the time has come for my departure. I have fought the good fight, I have finished the race, I have kept the faith. Now there is in store for me the crown of righteousness, which the Lord, the righteous Judge, will award to me on that day—and not only to me, but also to all who have longed for his appearing. [2 Timothy 4:6-8]

Paul sprinted to the finish line of life. He faced difficulties but remained faithful. He continued to serve God in the various circumstances. Now, at the end of his life he could rest. He had finished the work God had given him to do. It was time to go home.

Paul was like a builder building his own home. He faced cost overruns. He dealt with orders for supplies that were incomplete. He had to make adjustments when specifications were wrong. At times it was frustrating. At times he wanted to walk away. At times he thought about selling it all real cheap. But he didn't. He endured. He did the painstaking finish work. The house was complete. Now, it is time to move in. And when he walked through that front door of his home with his family, his joy was complete. The work was hard, but it was worth it. He was glad he didn't cut corners and didn't give up.

Paul finished the work. And that's the job that we have as well. The work may be hard, but it must be done before we can enjoy the reward of the Savior's "well done!" There may be pain to endure, setbacks to overcome, and changes to make. There may be times you want to walk away and say, "Forget it". But don't forget what is at the end of the journey. The work must be done. Be faithful, my friend. Hang on to the Father's hand and look for His smile in the clouds.

Practically Speaking

Paul's attitude toward life and death should be a model for our own attitude. I am not saying that loss won't be painful. It will be. I'm not saying that the uncertain character of what the transition of life to death involves won't scary. I'm betting it will be.

Parents who bury their children, Spouses who bury their mates, Children who bury their parents, will still face sadness. They will still ache. They will still wonder "what if". But in the midst of their sadness, there will the light of hope. That hope and confidence will come from the knowledge that this life is not all there is.

We know that some day this kind of pain will invade all of our lives. Some day we will face death. Our goal is to be prepared. To that end let me suggest three final things.

First, *be sure of your own salvation*. The hope of heaven is ONLY for Christians. If you have not turned to Christ as your only hope of eternal life, then you can have no real hope of Heaven and consequently you will know no real joy in difficult times. Your goodness cannot earn salvation for you; your parents cannot provide it for you; you have no hope apart from Christ.

So the first step then is to settle this issue. Turn away from trusting yourself and turn to Jesus. Confess your sin and your inability to earn salvation. Acknowledge Christ as God become man who has given his life for you. And then, rest and rely on what Christ has done for you. You must be His before you can know the hope of Heaven that yields joy in difficult times.

Put this book down and settle the issue if you haven't already done so. In simple faith and genuine commitment receive the gift of life. Maybe you might say something like this,

> *Lord Jesus, I am lost without you. I have run from you, ignored you, and fallen far short of your standards. I deserve nothing from you. Today I acknowledge and receive you as my Lord and Savior. I trust that your death on the cross was sufficient for my sin. I believe that as you rose literally from the dead, you will also raise me. I now set my sights on Heaven and look forward to the day when I can thank you in person.*

Second, *think about Heaven*. If you were planning a vacation to a new location you would get brochures, search the Internet, talk to travel agents. You would build your anticipation for the trip by learning everything you could about the location and what that location had to see and do.

In the same vein I encourage you to read a book or two about Heaven. Read the Biblical passages that speak of Heaven. Try to imagine the glory of that day. Create an appetite and a desire for that which is to come. The more you yearn for Heaven, the less you will fear what earth throws at you.

Third, *make the most of every opportunity now.* When times are not difficult we should be building our relationship with the Lord. We need to converse with God in prayer. We must be students of His promises and His directions. We must work at overcoming the sinful influences in our life. We must work together.

Perhaps it's time for you to make some changes so you can make better use of the time you have. Here are some suggestions,

- Eliminate some of the passive activity of your life (camping in front of a television, watching a movie, watching sporting events). You don't have to eliminate all these things, but make a real effort to cut down. Read more, engage others in conversation, get more rest, and learn something.

- Make it a point to notice people. We pass folks everyday who were sent to us by the Lord for us to encourage. Some of those people were sent to encourage us. We missed opportunities because we weren't paying attention. We need to open our eyes to life all the time!

- When planning your week's activities consider the ways you can serve and honor the Lord FIRST rather than last. Make worship an appointment that cannot be moved. Set aside time for Bible Study, for prayer, for calling on the sick and encouraging a friend. You know as well as I do that if you "fit these things in" you will find that you never get around to the eternal things.

- Use the telephone for ministry. Call that friend who is going through a rough time. Call the homebound person and let them know they are not forgotten. Call someone on the anniversary of the death of his or her spouse and tell them, "I remember too". Call someone up and share a spiritual insight. It doesn't have to be a long call to be effective and helpful.

Think of how many lives you could touch if you set aside one half hour a couple times a week just to call people. You would bring joy to others and find it yourself.

I suggest these things not so we can get to Heaven. Jesus took care of providing our way to Heaven. It is my hope that we will do these things so we will be ready when the tough times enter our lives. At those times I hope you and I will be deeply rooted. So deep, in fact that we can face any situation with the resolve that "to live is Christ, to die is gain."

Study Questions
1. When do you think are the most difficult times to be joyful?
2. What is the right perspective on death and how does this perspective change the way we face,
    a. The loss of someone we love?
    b. A disappointing medical report?
    c. A job setback?
    d. Economic hardship?
3. What do you think it means to "live for Christ"? How can you do this without becoming a Pastor or missionary?
4. What items would you add to the list of things we can do to "make the most of every opportunity?"
5. What books have you read about Heaven? What did you learn?
6. What one suggestion from this chapter will you work on right away?

4

The Focus Needed for a Life of Joy

Philippians 1:27-30

Have you ever had the experience of starting to pull out into an intersection only to be startled by a car right in front of you? You are sure that you looked both ways and you know you didn't see the car coming. It happens to all of us (or at least I hope so). We know that we must have *seen* the car but for some reason what we saw didn't "register" in our consciousness. The reason it didn't register was because of a lack of focus on our part. We were not anticipating any traffic and so we didn't see any traffic. We were driving, but our mind was elsewhere.

It happens to us all the time. We walk through a store and walk right past our best friends without even seeing them. If you are distracted enough you can walk through the living room of your home and not see your family sitting there.

Perhaps you have noticed this lack of focus in your devotional life. You sit down to read a passage of Scripture and several paragraphs into your reading you realize that you have no idea what you have just read. You read the words, but not really. We begin to pray with all sincerity, but before we know it, our mind is someplace else.

If we want to be good at anything we have to learn to focus. It's true for athletes, it's true for construction workers, and it is true for accountants, musicians, and teachers. It should be no great revelation then to announce that those who want to live the joyful life must be focused also. Paul calls for Christ focused living in these words,

> *Whatever happens, conduct yourselves in a manner worthy of the gospel of Christ. Then, whether I come and see you or only hear about you in my absence, I will know that you stand firm in one spirit, contending as one man for the faith of the gospel without being frightened in any way by those who oppose you. This is a sign to them that they will be destroyed, but that you will be saved—and that by God. For it has been granted to you on behalf of Christ not only to believe on him, but also to suffer for him, since you are going through the same struggle you saw I had, and now hear that I still have.* [Philippians 1:27-30]

Before we can know joy, we must sharpen our focus. The Greek word used for "conduct yourself" is a word used for conducting yourself properly as a citizen. When an Ambassador from one country is sent to another country they are told to remember that they represent their homeland. They should act in a way that brings honor, not disgrace to their country.

I hear this same idea coming from a principal or coach when they say to their students or team, "you represent your school, or community . . . represent them well."

I remember a high school football game my son was involved in. Our small town school played a powerful Chicago team. The attitude of the Chicago players was one of scorn for the "country hicks". Our team heard some of their comments and our coach (a master of motivation) used that to his advantage. He told the players that they had something to prove. He told them that they represented their entire community. They went out on the field and won a stirring (and exciting) victory. They conducted themselves in a manner worthy of the entire community.

Paul says in 2 Corinthians 5 that God has made us His ambassadors . . . as if He was making His appeal through us (v. 20). We represent our Savior,

- when we are at work
- when we are negotiating a contract
- when we are at the complaint desk of a store
- when we are having a frustrating day on the golf course
- when we are mad at our spouse or children
- when we are managing our personal finances
- when we are involved in an athletic event (and things are getting tense)
- when we are going out for a night of entertainment
- when we are driving on a crowded highway

No matter where you are . . . you represent Jesus. Paul's counsel is simple: Represent Him Well.

What the Spiritually Focused Life Will Do

Paul described the kinds of things that characterize a focused life. First, those living the focused life will **Stand Fast**. Focused people aren't tossed about by the latest fads. In the storms of life these people stand firm.

We will have to stand firm to hold our ground. As believers we will face opposition from many fronts. We will be attacked by competing philosophies. We will face opposition from the values and morals of the world. People who disagree with us will insult us and try to get us to waver. Everywhere we turn we face those who wish to weaken our foundations. The one who lives consistent with the gospel, is a person who is standing firm in the midst of opposition. The person who loses his or her focus is ripe for a fall.

In order to stand, we must be anchored to the right place. If you try to hang a heavy picture on the wall you can't just drive a nail arbitrarily into the wall (I speak from personal experience). It may hold for a while . . . but if the nail is not anchored to some solid support, it will eventually work itself out of the wall.

This is why it is important for us to take the time to make sure we understand who Jesus is, what He did, how we find salvation, and what the Bible teaches. I know lots of people who say, "I don't want theology or doctrine . . . I just want to follow Jesus!" It sounds pious but it is one of the most foolish things I have ever heard anyone say. You can't follow Jesus unless you can recognize the Savior from the host of counterfeits in the world. And you can't talk about who the true Jesus is without engaging in theology and doctrine.

Second, those who are focused and conducting themselves in a manner worthy of the gospel will **Contend as One.** The word for "contend as one" is the Greek word sun-athleo. It is the word from which we get our word "athletic". Just as a team must work together to be victorious, so Paul feels the church needs to work together to be successful in the world. It is the idea of working as a team.

I love the film, REMEMBER THE TITANS. It is the true story of two coaches, one white and one black who are told to coach a newly integrated team. The head coach (Played by Denzel Washington) has the job of trying to get this team to put aside their differences and focus on their common goal. It was not an easy job. Slowly but surely the players began to see people, rather than skin color. As the team began to play as a team, they began to play good football . . . and more importantly they began to change. And their change brought a divided community together.

In like manner, in the church we come from different backgrounds. We have different tastes, styles and interests. We can let our differences divide us or we can let our common experience of grace in Christ unite us. Yes, in the quest for truth we may still debate issues . . . . but our goal will not be to be "right", but to know Christ better. Our differences will not be the cause for division . . . they will provide opportunities to grow.

Christians fighting Christians only causes the world to turn away. When Christians work together, the world takes notice. In the early church many people didn't understand the gospel, but they did understand that the people of the church loved each other. Does the world see this today? If we are focused and conducting ourselves in a manner worthy of the gospel we will gladly set aside our ego for the purpose of advancing the Kingdom of God. We will cooperate rather than separate.

The third characteristic of the focused life is **An Absence of Fear.** Again, the Greek word that Paul uses helps us to understand his point. The word for "fear" is the same word that would be used for a horse that was startled. A startled horse takes off running. Christians living in a manner worthy of the gospel will not run away out of fear.

Do I ever feel afraid? Of course I do. This is one of the points of struggle in my life as well as yours. When bills are coming due and the bank account is empty we are sometimes afraid. When we have to walk into a new situation we may be afraid of the unknown. When we have a close call on the highway fear wells up within us. When the Doctor tells us the news "isn't good" fear begins to rise. As we are rolled into an operating room, we may feel an apprehension that is born from a fear of an unknown outcome. When our loved one lays close to death, the thought of a future without that person may make us afraid. We are all afraid on occasion.

The challenge for the child of God is to regain our focus as quickly as possible. Our God is sufficient for our needs. He has guaranteed us life beyond the grave. He has promised to help us. When we remember whom we belong to, we find the fear will slip away.

Truths that Help us Focus

It sounds so simple doesn't it? But it's not. Paul indicates that this kind of focus has to do with our attitude. There are two things we need to constantly remember..

First, we must remember that we are **Privileged To Believe.**

A soldier feels a special sense of pride when they don the uniform of their country. If you talk to most who have served their country, they still have their uniforms somewhere. They may not be able to button that coat or close those pants . . . but they still have the uniforms. Why? Old soldiers keep their uniforms because it was a special honor to wear the same uniform that so many have worn in defense of our country. It is an honor to serve your country. Every time you see that uniform in your closet, you remember with pride.

In like manner, those of us who wear the name of Christ should realize what a privilege and honor it is to be called a child of God.

- It is an honor to be given a gift as wonderful as forgiveness and eternal life
- It is an honor to be granted eternal access to the Father.
- It is an honor to trust and be associated with one who is so trustworthy.
- It is an honor to commit our cares to one who is sufficient for our every need.
- It is an honor to serve one who never takes us for granted

We must always remember the privilege that comes from following Christ. We must never take it lightly. When we begin thinking of an honor as a "duty" we will begin to resist. When we begin to think of an honor as "a right" we begin to demand. We stand in a grace that we do not deserve. We have been given a position we will never be worthy to receive. The honor we have been given should make us more determined than ever to live up to that honor. We should live every moment with gratitude.

The second attitude . . . is much more difficult to accept. Paul tells us that we should see **Suffering as a Privilege** How foreign this is to our ears! Many people flock to Christianity because they believe it will end their suffering! And indeed it does . . . on one level. When we come to Christ we no longer have to fret about eternity. When we come to Christ the torment in our soul is taken care of. But our struggle with the world may just be beginning.

When we stand with Jesus Christ we are standing against the current of public opinion. We may suffer the pangs of persecution because what we believe doesn't square with popular opinion.

- We believe there is ONE not many ways to Heaven
- We believe in a literal heaven and hell
- We believe there is an absolute standard of truth (the Bible)
- We believe in a Sovereign God who has created all things and sustains all things

These alone will bring plenty of hostility in your direction. Try standing up for these beliefs in a biology class at a state university.

Try proclaiming one of these truths on one of the daily talk shows. Put these beliefs into practice on the floor of the factory. You will find that people do not like the message of Christianity. They will strike out at us no matter how sincere we may be.

Try to understand how suffering could be seen as a privilege. Suppose you have a child who is in desperate health. As a parent, you would willingly endure personal suffering on behalf of your child. You would go without sleep. You would sacrifice a body part. You would spend your life savings. You would even give up your own life if it could save your child. And if someone asked you, you'd tell them that you would do it all again because of your love. Sacrifice gives us a chance to express love in a bold fashion.

This is the way Paul loved Christ. And this is the way we should love Him too. We should love Him enough to suffer anything for the honor of His name. It is not a curse any more than being a parent is a curse. It is a privilege to be able to demonstrate our love for our Savior. What an honor to be identified as one of his followers. After all He has done on our behalf it is really a small price pay in comparison.

Paul saw the handwriting on the wall. He sensed that the Philippians might soon be persecuted for their faith. Stephen had already been killed (with Paul's help) and James had been put to death. In AD 67, Nero ordered the burning of Rome. The fire lasted for nine days and when the blame turned to Nero, Nero blamed the Christians. Nero came at the Christians with a new vengeance. He contrived all manner of punishments for the Christians that only the most infernal imagination could design. In particular, he had some sewed up in skins of wild beasts, and then they were attacked by dogs until they expired; others were dressed in shirts made stiff with wax, were fixed to stakes, and set on fire in his gardens, in order to illuminate them. This persecution was general throughout the whole Roman Empire. In the course of it, St. Paul and St. Peter were martyred.

In Hebrews 11 we read this account that early believers
*[they] were tortured and refused to be released, so
that they might gain a better resurrection. Some
faced jeers and flogging, while still others were*

chained and put in prison. They were stoned; they were sawed in two; they were put to death by the sword. They went about in sheepskins and goatskins, destitute, persecuted and mistreated—the world was not worthy of them. (Heb. 11:35-38)

In each case, the people considered it an honor to suffer for His name. Do you still find that an odd statement? Think about those who consider it an honor to serve their country in a war. Think about firemen and policemen who consider it an honor to risk their lives to save another. When any of these folks die they are called heroes. They are buried with honor.

I have done hundreds of funerals over the years. And I have witnessed scores of military burials. When "Taps" is played, the flag is folded, the salute is sounded, and that flag is presented to a family member, it is a moving moment. It means something to have served and to serve well.

We hope we will never have to suffer as are forefathers did. But even if we do, we should pray that we would face those times with honor, character and dignity. Hopefully, we will never be thrown in prison or covered with animal skins. But we may face more subtle suffering and persecution for our faith.

- we may lose our job
- we may face lawsuits
- we may be ostracized and verbally abused
- we may be physically attacked
- we may face business losses
- we may be asked to do more work than others
- we may be ignored by people we wish noticed us
- we may be discriminated against because of our profession of faith.

Whatever suffering we may face, it is important to make sure that it is coming from being united with Christ (and not from our arrogance, stupidity or laziness). We should count it a privilege to stand up for Him.

The Results of Focused Living

Paul points to two immediate results of focused living. First, <u>We will Verify Our Salvation.</u> The world looks at how we handle the tough times to find out whether or not our profession of faith is real or not. Jesus told his disciples in the Sermon on the Mount that the way to distinguish true prophets from false prophets is by the way they live. I think Jesus would say the same is true of believers. A true believer shows their genuineness by the life they live.

We verify the truthfulness of our salvation when we live consistent with our profession. If we say we believe we are forgiven, we should live as people who have been set free from our past. If we say we are saved by God's undeserved grace, we should be gracious in our dealings with others. If we say we believe in the dreadfulness of sin, then we should hate sin and work tirelessly to overcome it in our lives. If we say we believe in the future glory of Heaven then we should show that our longing is not for this world, but the next. We do that by the way we use our time, spend our money, and the attention we give to developing a relationship with Christ. If we believe God will supply all our needs we should stop churning. If we believe God is working in every situation, then we should show joyful endurance even in the hard times.

If you don't see these kinds of changes in your life . . . it is important that you ask whether you have *really* trusted Him at all. Being saved is more than a prayer you say after a moving talk . . . being saved is a settled trust and commitment to what Christ has done on your behalf. True commitment reveals itself in the way we live.

The second effect of Living in a manner worthy of the Gospel is <u>we will see others won to Christ.</u> There is nothing that helps a person see the lack in the own life . . . like seeing the blessing in the life of another. People of the world take notice of the emptiness that is in their own lives when they see the peace, joy, and contentment that exist in the child of God.

Jesus told his disciples,

> *"You are the light of the world. A city on a hill cannot be hidden. Neither do people light a lamp and put it under a bowl. Instead they put it on its*

stand, and it gives light to everyone in the house. In the same way, let your light shine before men, that they may see your good deeds and praise your Father in heaven. [Matthew 5:14-16]

When we live consistent with the gospel of Jesus Christ, our light shines and others can see . . . and will be drawn to the truth.

Practically Speaking

So, having said all this, what do we do now? I have some suggestions. First, we must take the time to reflect on the privilege and honor that is ours in being children of God. Many of us have grown up in the church. We take it for granted. Others have been believers for a good long time and we have forgotten where we were and where we were headed when he found us. So, take some time to consider where you might be today if it weren't for His wonderful grace. Think about what your future would hold and all the things you would have missed. Focus on the blessing that is yours to know Christ personally.

Second, do a personal inventory of your life. What practices are inconsistent with the gospel of Christ? What behaviors dishonor his name? Be honest. It's going to hurt, but it is necessary. Look at your vocabulary, your thought life, your passions, and your priorities. Look at the way you are at church and compare it to the way you are with your friends. Is there inconsistency there? Make the necessary changes. When you do, your fellowship with God will be richer and your joy will be greater.

Third, find some way to remind yourself that you represent Jesus. Maybe you could hang a Bible verse that says, "you are Christ's Ambassadors as though God were making His appeal through us." [2 Cor. 5:20] in a strategic spot.

Maybe you could put a little sign on your mirror that says, "Will people see Christ in me today?" Perhaps you could choose to wear a cross or carry your Bible with you. Whatever you choose as a reminder, consciously use it to keep focused on the fact that your purpose is to live a life worthy of the gospel. You want to represent Him well.

Finally, make your ability to focus a matter of prayer. Ask God to help you live out the gospel wherever you are. Ask Him to help you to reflect His goodness to others. Be honest about your areas of struggle and ask for His help. Ask Him to change your attitude.

As you and I learn to live with a godly focus, we will love God more. We will also be more consistent and enthusiastic in our living. We will know a greater sense of joy. And we will be better equipped to see the oncoming traffic.

Discussion Questions

1. Who was an inspiration to you as you were first beginning in the Christian life? Why was this person so inspiring?
2. What time of day do you have the most difficulty focusing? Why do you think that is?
3. On a scale of 1 to 10 (1 being high) how do you rate your spiritual focus? How conscious are you of your representation of Christ in everything you do?
4. Of the three characteristics of what a focused believer looks like, which characteristic is most lacking in your life? What steps can you take to strengthen that area of your discipleship?
5. Do you understand the parental and military illustrations about the privilege of suffering? Can you think of other examples that would help us to understand this notion of the privilege of suffering?
6. How does focused living verify our salvation? How is this different from "earning" our salvation?

5

The Surprising Ingredient
for Joyful Living

Philippians 2:1-4

Deep down inside of us there is an ache for an illusive happiness, or joy, that seems just out of reach. We want the joy the apostle Paul had. Most of the time we seem to think that we will find this joy only if we can,

- master some method
- conquer some obstacle
- reach some pinnacle
- make some purchase
- refine some personality trait

But in all the lists we might make that include the steps to joyful living most people would never include the key ingredient the apostle Paul listed. Listen to what Paul tells us in Philippians 2,

If you have any encouragement from being united with Christ, if any comfort from his love, if any fellowship with the Spirit, if any tenderness and compassion, then make my joy complete by being like-minded, having the same love, being one in

*spirit and purpose. Do nothing out of selfish ambi-
tion or vain conceit, but in humility consider others
better than yourselves. Each of you should look not
only to your own interests, but also to the interests of
others.* [Philippians 2:1-4]

Paul suggests that those who are true believers will work
together; love each other; and serve each other. In fact, this servant
attitude is the key to our unity and the finest expression of our love.
Did you have "develop a servant heart" on your list of things that
were needed to find joy? I didn't either.

The servant attitude runs counter to the attitude our culture
seems to encourage. We are challenged to "climb the mountain of
success" and to not let "anyone stand in your way". Aggressiveness
is really the order of the day. Our society is filled with pushers not
givers. In fact, a person with a servant heart is often seen as weak, a
person who is going to be "used" by others, and lacking in ambition. Could it be that this increasingly aggressive attitude is directly
related to the growing lack of joylessness?

I think that is exactly the conclusion we are to draw. Joy comes
from adopting the servant attitude of Jesus. Before we can become
servants, however, we have to understand what being a servant
means.

IT MEANS WE GIVE BEFORE WE GRAB

I realize that this sounds kind of crass . . . but it is the right
picture. We spend a good portion of our life looking out for
ourselves. We are constantly pushing and grabbing. Let's face it;
it's the American Way. We are raised believing that the one who is
more forceful is the one who gets the most power. But this is a
myth.

The Bible tells us that the servant is the one who will be most
exalted. The servant is the one who is honored by God. The servant
is the one who is most likely to reach others with the gospel. But
servanthood is difficult.

Is it just me or do you see your aggressiveness come out when
you are in a crowd? I remember when I lived in Chicago. There was

a real science involved with pushing your way forward in a crowd. I had a strategy for coming home from Seminary at the beginning of "rush hour" (the time when no one rushes anywhere). There is a spot on the highway near O'Hare airport where at least twelve toll-booths empty into four lanes of traffic (what were they thinking?). At "rush hour" you needed a strategy and I had one. As long as I was in one particular lane I knew I could keep moving forward and "edge everyone else out."

You can see this same aggressiveness in the lines at Wal-Mart or other stores. If you are like me, you plan a strategy to get to the shortest line before everyone else does. I've been to high school football games where people came hours before the game so they could stake out their seats with blankets, cushions, and other items (and then they went home!). This was all to keep the other guy from taking "their" spot.

Have you ever gone to a day after Thanksgiving sale at a large mall? Yikes! A person could get killed in the mad rush to get wrapping paper for half price!

These are the telltale signs of the "selfish ambition" that Paul talks about. In these settings the only person that matters is ME. But it is not just in crowds . . . we seek to grab the spotlight, the credit, the advantage in many areas. .

- We trumpet our good deeds so the world will applaud us
- We perform our good deeds so the world will notice us
- We gravitate to those who can enhance our position and drift from those who may "stain" our reputation
- We monopolize a conversation so the spotlight will remain on us
- Our prayers are consumed with arguments as to why God should give us what we want
- Anyone not driving the same speed as we are on the highway is considered "an idiot"
- Anyone who does not see things as we do is "stupid"

In order to have a servant heart, we must fight the aggressive and selfish tendencies in ourselves. We must ask the Lord to change us, to help us see beyond ourselves, to become soft rather than hard, generous rather than selfish, and giving rather than grabbing.

OUR GOAL IS TO SERVE GOD AND NOT OURSELVES

Rather than seek our own glory and pursue our own agenda, the servant of God is concerned about only one thing . . . honoring the Lord. The true servant doesn't care if they get the credit as long as God gets the honor.

It's similar to the way things are in athletics. If you play on a team, the goal must be the team and not the individual. Sometimes the running back must block. Sometimes the big hitter needs to sacrifice so the runner can advance a base and get into scoring position. Sometimes the star shooter has to pass the ball to a teammate. The goal is the team.

Business experts tell us that you can 't be effective or successful unless you know what your goal is. Once you have your goal, everything and everyone must be working toward reaching that goal.

What is the goal of the Christian life? What is the goal of your church? Is it seeking fame, fortune, comfort, and pleasure? Are we pursuing "decisions", baptisms, and new members? The true goal is to bring honor to Christ and to bring as many people to receive and follow Christ as possible.

If we want to reach this goal then we must serve Christ and serve each other. If our goal is to honor the Lord and lead others to Him, then we will need to adapt our desires to His. If our goal is His glory then we should be willing to work in the shadows. We will be willing to do whatever is needed to further His Kingdom.

WE WILL WORK ON OUR FAILURES RATHER THAN CRITICIZE THE FAILURE OF OTHERS

Paul says the servant will "consider others to be better than ourselves." The principle is not hard to understand. We are not to consider others better than us because of their race, their socio-economic status, their gender, their experience or their age. It is not a matter of externals. We are to consider others better than ourselves because though we don't know the heart of another person, we do know our heart.

We are to be fierce and painfully honest in looking at our lives while giving the benefit of the doubt for others. I know I often do things for selfish motives. I know that my thoughts sometimes are not honoring to God. I know I have been manipulative in my methods. I know that sometimes I do things only *because* others are looking.

We live by a double standard. We want others to attribute to us the best possible motives for everything we do, and we want people to always give us another chance. Our plea for mercy is tempered with the words, "but I didn't mean it" (even though often we know that is exactly what we meant). And if we are honest we will admit that often at the very time we are asking for charity, we are quick to impugn the motives of others. We want others to give us a break, but we are often unwilling to extend that same "break" to other people.

Do you remember the parable of the unjust servant? A man was brought before the King because of a large debt that was unpaid. The debtor pleaded with the King to extend mercy. The King forgave the huge debt. The man was elated and relieved. He felt that God had smiled upon him.

On the way home this same forgiven man met a man who owed him a much smaller amount of money. He confronted the man about his debt. The debtor asked for a little more time and an extension of mercy (the very thing this forgiven man had earlier asked from the King).

You would have thought that this man who had freshly been forgiven would be glad to extend mercy to another. But he refused to extend mercy and had the man arrested and thrown in debtor's prison.

This man was governed by a double standard. He wanted mercy from the King but was unwilling to extend it to another. He wanted one standard for his sin while applying another standard to the sins of others.

I have to admit that I see this double standard in my life all the time. I want people to consider the hard day I've had when I snap at them. I want them to realize that I am acting out of frustration rather than malice. Yet I know I show very little patience with those who might be in the same situation as me. I think those people should "be more careful" or they should "get themselves under control." I am not willing to extend to others what I want for myself. The principle is simple: I need work on my attitudes before I try to fix yours! Let me give some other examples,

- I give someone a hard time and they are offended. I want them to understand that I was "only kidding". But when someone continues to "needle me" about something, I get angry and feel justified when I strike out at them.
- When I am driving somewhere but I don't know where I am going I want other people to be patient and understanding. However, when I am behind someone like this, I am anything but patient.
- When a family member spends a little money on something for their enjoyment I call it wasteful. When I do it, I am just "enjoying my hard-earned money".
- When I arrive somewhere late I want people to understand that I was "unavoidably detained" but when others are late I tend to think of them as inconsiderate.
- I want people to be able to sense when I am "in the middle of something" and wait for a more convenient time to talk with me. However, I often will barge right in on others without giving a thought to what they are doing.

No matter how you look at it, it is a double standard. The true servant is the one who treats other people, as they want to be treated.

The true servant is so aware of his/her own spiritual state that they would never presume to point their finger at another. They are so humbled by God's grace that they are eager and willing to extend that grace to others.

Please understand, I'm not saying that we are to overlook the sinful behaviors in the lives of those around us. We must not shrug off the affair, addiction, dishonesty, or other sin of our friend by saying, "who am I to judge." It is not up to us to judge these things because God has already done so. If we love our friends we will confront them with the sin in their lives just like we need our friends to do to us. What I am talking about are those petty things that divide churches, families, and communities.

WE WILL NOTICE THE NEED THAT OTHERS HAVE

Paul said, "Each of you should look not only to your own interests, but also to the interests of others." The servant of God is aware of those around him. He or she notices the struggles that others are going through.

Much of the time we are so aware that *we* are present that we don't even notice that others are present too. We are so wrapped up with our needs, our impressions, and our goals, that we don't have time to consider others. But the servant is different.

I remember a Tract that I read when I was a kid, it was called, "Holy Joe". It was a little comic book that told the story of a Christian man who went into the service. He wouldn't swear like the rest of the guys and they made fun of him. When he got up early in the morning to pray the men hurled insults at him. One morning they all threw their boots at him. But when these soldiers later woke up, their boots were polished and put in their place. The servant heart of the soldier eventually won the hearts of the other soldiers. This soldier knew that it was his job to show the love of Christ to these men and he did so not by force but by his servant attitude.

James Boice tells of a Christian who lived in China. He was a poor rice farmer, and his fields lay high on a mountain. Every day he pumped water into the paddies of new rice, and every morning he returned to find that a neighbor who lived down the hill had opened the dikes surrounding the Christian's field to let the water fill his own. For a while the Christian ignored the injustice, but at last he became desperate. He met and prayed with other Christians and came up with this solution. The next day the Christian farmer rose early in the morning and first filled his neighbor's fields; then he attended to his own. The neighbor subsequently became a Christian, his unbelief overcome by a genuine demonstration of a Christian's humility and Christlike character.[2]

This is true servanthood. It is caring for another. It is learning to listen with your eyes, your ears, and your heart. It is putting service before rights, and ministry before convenience. It's an attitude. And this attitude comes from the transformation Christ brings.

WE WILL FOLLOW THE EXAMPLE OF JESUS

If we want to know what a true servant looks like, we need to look no further than Jesus. Paul writes,

> *Your attitude should be the same as that of Christ Jesus:*
>
> *Who, being in very nature God, did not consider equality with God something to be grasped, but made himself nothing, taking the very nature of a servant, being made in human likeness. And being found in appearance as a man, He humbled himself and became obedient to death—even death on a cross!*

This is a wonderfully rich passage that teaches much about the deity of Christ. For the purpose of our study, look at these words and see the example of servanthood that we are given.

Jesus, even though He was God, did not consider equality with God something to be grasped. These are difficult words but I believe Paul is telling us that Jesus refused to think only of the privileges that were rightfully his. Instead of refusing to go to earth and be a human because it was (literally) beneath Him, he set aside His rights and privileges so He could be our redeemer.

Not only did Jesus set aside his rights and powers as God . . . He became a servant. He took human form and ministered to those who owed Him worship. He cared for those who had ignored Him and rebelled against Him.

But he didn't stop here. He became a sacrifice. Jesus willingly surrendered his life so that you and I might be forgiven and have the opportunity to live forever in Heaven. He gave His life for the very people who treated Him shamefully.

I shudder to think of how things would have been different if Jesus had my attitudes. I'm sobered to think that I might have responded to the Father's plan of redemption by saying, "Forget those rebels! Let them destroy themselves. We can always create other worlds." I'm sure I would have resisted. In fact, I'm pretty sure I would have refused to give myself for such ungrateful people.

The attitude of Jesus does not come naturally.

Whenever you feel like you are making too great a sacrifice, think about Jesus. When you wonder why you are always the one that has to be the one to give, think about what Jesus gave for you. In those times when you feel it won't do any good to serve another, remember the one who gave His life for your redemption and the change His sacrifice has made in your life. If you really want to be like Jesus, you start by being a servant.

Practically Speaking

The surprising formula for joyful living is simple: if you want to know joy, give of yourself to the Lord and to those around you. Perhaps you have heard that the word joy stands for: Jesus first; Others second; Yourself third.

It seems like an odd prescription, doesn't it? But if you think about your life, you will see the wisdom of what is being said. Haven't some of the most satisfying times of your life been those times when you freely gave of yourself to a project without any concern about what others would say? It may have been a time you visited someone who was sick. Or maybe it was the sweet satisfaction that came from making a quiet contribution to a project that brought joy to another. Wasn't there a deep joy in those times? Didn't you discover a satisfaction unlike anything you have found before?

May I give some simple suggestions for how we might cultivate a servant heart?

- Remind yourself how foreign the servant heart is to your nature. Make servanthood and humility an issue you deliberately think about. Bring the matter to the front of your mind. Make it an issue of focused prayer.
- Constantly work at being a giver rather than a taker. Pick up that paper lying on the sidewalk (rather than pretending you don't see it), do the dishes, take out the garbage (instead of balancing one more item on top), help someone clean up without being asked, change the toilet paper roll, take time to listen, and do what will please another without whining about it or resisting it.
- Give up an evening to help another with a project. The most

precious gift we have is "time". Give someone the gift of time.

- Rake a neighbor's lawn, cut their grass, or shovel the snow off their walk.
- Stop and talk with someone on the road (and act like you have nothing else you need to do).
- Do some act of kindness . . . and then tell no one. (That's the hardest for me.)
- •Be alert to a burden that another is carrying and then do something tangible to lighten their load (do some of their chores, run one of their errands, make a meal).
- Give up what you want to do to do something for another.

None of these things will be easy. We will need to work to develop the servant mindset.Can you imagine the change that could take place if even Christian people began to demonstrate a servant's heart? There would be fewer conflicts and less hurting and lonely people in the world. People would like each other more. The world would see Jesus in action in us. And I think the world would be so attracted to what they see that our sanctuaries would be full. People would recognize that there is something different about us. They would recognize that we actually seemed to care. And then they might even come to believe that God cares too . . . and who knows, they might even turn to the one who will lead them to Heaven in the world to come . . . and to the joy of servanthood in the present.

Discussion Questions

1. What examples can you think of from this last week where you saw the selfish aggressive human spirit of contemporary society?
2. Why do you think the servant mentality is so foreign to contemporary living?
3. Which part of the servant heart would you find most difficult to practice?
    a. Giving before we grab?
    b. Serving God rather than yourself?
    c. Addressing our failures rather than the failures of others?
    d. Noticing the needs of those around us?

4. There is a list at the end of the chapter of some practical things that we could do to begin to cultivate an attitude of servanthood. What additional items would you add to the list?
5. Do some reading in Servanthood. You might begin by reading *Descending into Greatness* by Bill Hybels or *Improving Your Serve* by Charles Swindoll. Read these books for further suggestions on how to develop the servant heart.

6

Giving Christ His Rightful Place

Philippians 2:9-11

Every four years, January 20th is a special day for the United States of America because on that day a President is sworn into office for a new term. The day is filled with pomp and circumstance (by American standards). There are gala balls and grand celebrations. Inauguration Day is the culmination of a long campaign and the beginning of a new administration.

In one sense this is the perfect contemporary analogy for Philippians 2:9-11. In these verses Paul points to the ultimate inauguration; the inauguration of the Ruler of the Universe.

> *Therefore God exalted him to the highest place and gave him the name that is above every name, that at the name of Jesus every knee should bow, in heaven and on earth and under the earth, and every tongue confess that Jesus Christ is Lord, to the glory of God the Father.* (Phil. 2:9-11)

These verses are important to our pursuit of joy because they remind us why Jesus is the one qualified to lead us to joy. We need to be crystal clear whom it is that we follow and serve. So, let me share just a few observations with you about the heavenly inauguration.

JESUS DESERVES THE POSITION HE RECEIVED

Paul begins with the word "therefore" which means it is a conclusion or a consequence of what has been stated previously. So, it is because of the role that Christ played as servant and Savior that He is exalted. He deserves and has earned the honor He receives.

Jesus has proved Himself to be the perfect Son of God. He has proved His holiness by His obedience. He has proved His love by His willing death for sinful human beings. Let's not forget that He died for us when we didn't show any inclination toward Him. He has proved His power by His resurrection and by His ability to change human hearts. Jesus has proved that He has the best interest of God's created in mind because He willingly left His heavenly position and took the form of a servant so that He might rescue and redeem us.

Jesus deserves His position as exalted Ruler of the World. By contrast, let me state the obvious. We do not deserve this position. We have proved over and over again that we are often only concerned about others to the degree that they can help us. Jesus died for sin . . . we committed it. We sent Him to the cross. Even on our best days we could never deserve the position that Christ has earned.

Now here's the tough question . . . if it is obvious that Christ has earned his position and equally apparent that we do not deserve that position . . . why is it that we spend so much of our time trying to play God?

- We ignore or modify the guidelines He's given. We decide which commands are "relevant" and worthy of our obedience.
- We demand God work by our timetable rather than rest in His
- We think our wisdom is better than His in the circumstances of life
- We presume to judge Him and call Him, "unfair", "unjust", "arbitrary", "insensitive"

- We usurp His role by judging each other even though we don't have all the information.
- At times we are even guilty of trying to "save" people through our methods and manipulation rather than by pointing them to the Savior.

In each of these cases we challenge our Lord's rightful position. When we act in these ways we are attempting to overthrow His position as the Ruler of the World. It is an act of a fool.

JESUS IS GIVEN THE PREEMINENT POSITION

"Therefore God exalted him to the highest place and gave him the name that is above every name",

Most would agree that the name that Jesus is "given" is the title "Lord". The word "Lord" is used three ways in the New Testament. It is used sometimes as a polite form of address. It would be like you and I addressing a superior as "sir". Second it is used for the master of a slave. Maybe it would be the equivalent of our "boss". It refers to a person who has authority over another. The third way the title Lord was used is as a title for God.

All around us people use the name "Lord" in these three ways. Some people call Him the "Lord Jesus" as a title similar to "Prince Charles". Others refer to Jesus as Lord because they see Jesus as a great leader among men. Both of these groups of people sound like Christians while in reality they are not. When a Christian calls Jesus Lord they are acknowledging Him as God and as the one who has supreme authority in our lives and circumstances. They are confessing Him as the one who rules over all. He has the final say in EVERY area of life.

Before the first century came to a close, the Roman Empire demanded that Christians acknowledge Caesar as Lord. Many Christians went to their death rather than say, "Caesar is Lord." This was a title that was reserved for Christ alone.

Take a minute and ask yourself an honest question: Which way do you use the title "Lord"? Do you recognize Him as the ruler and giver of life? Is He in the supreme position in your life and heart? Or is "lord" merely a title to you?

Notice one more thing: WE do not declare that Jesus is Lord . . .

God does. God gives Him this position. So Jesus is Lord whether you recognize it or not. He has God-given authority. He is not waiting to be declared Lord. He has already been declared Lord. He IS the Lord. The question for you and me is whether we will bow before His Lordship.

ULTIMATELY EVERYONE WILL ACKNOWLEDGE HIS LORDSHIP

> *That at the name of Jesus every knee should bow, in heaven and on earth and under the earth, and every tongue confess that Jesus Christ is Lord, to the glory of God the Father.* [10-11]

The third thing to notice is that there is coming a day when *everyone* will acknowledge Christ as Lord. We read that EVERY knee will bow. No one will be excluded from this group. This group will include those in Heaven and those on earth. It will include the spiritual world as well as the human world. There will be those who speak these words with joy . . .and there will be those who speak these words with sorrow.

Remember my earlier illustration of the Presidential election? It doesn't matter who you liked or voted for in the general election. On January 20 every citizen must acknowledge the one inaugurated as President. To some the words will be bitter. To others they will be sweet. But everyone will have to recognize the position of the one inaugurated.

At the inauguration of Jesus, the angels and the demons will both acknowledge the rightful Lordship of Christ. The saved and the lost will acknowledge this Lordship. All that is in nature and in Heaven will bow before His sovereignty. But it will not be a joyful day for everyone.

When Christ is acknowledged as the Lord of Life and as the rightful ruler there will be no suggestion that a recount would change anything. Everyone will know that the declaration is true and appropriate. But this does not mean that everyone will be a Christian. It does not mean that everyone will go to Heaven. Jesus told us,

"Not everyone who says to me, 'Lord, Lord,' will enter the kingdom of heaven, but only he who does the will of my Father who is in heaven. Many will say to me on that day, 'Lord, Lord, did we not prophesy in your name, and in your name drive out demons and perform many miracles?' Then I will tell them plainly, 'I never knew you. Away from me, you evildoers!'

"Therefore everyone who hears these words of mine and puts them into practice is like a wise man who built his house on the rock. The rain came down, the streams rose, and the winds blew and beat against that house; yet it did not fall, because it had its foundation on the rock. But everyone who hears these words of mine and does not put them into practice is like a foolish man who built his house on sand. The rain came down, the streams rose, and the winds blew and beat against that house, and it fell with a great crash." [Matthew 7:21-27]

These are important words to hear. Jesus says it is not the words that we say that matter. It is not whether *we* recognize Him . . . but whether *He* recognizes *us* as one of His true followers.

I can tell you that I met Dr. James Kennedy, a prominent television Pastor. And I would be telling you the truth. I could tell you that I talked with Dr. Kennedy and would also be telling you the truth. But could I say that Dr. Kennedy knows me? No. In fact, I'm sure that if you asked Dr. Kennedy what he thought of Bruce Goettsche, Dr. Kennedy would say, "Bruce Who?"

I did have a passing conversation with James Kennedy at a conference. But that is not a relationship. And the test on the final day will be: Did we have a passing encounter with Jesus or a relationship with Him? Those who have a relationship with Christ will enter into eternal life. Those who only had a passing encounter with Him (or none at all), will be cast out of His presence. You see, declaring that Christ is Lord and submitting to His Lordship are two different things.

We do not need to wonder if one day we will acknowledge Jesus Christ as Lord. We will. There is no question on that issue. The question is whether we will be acknowledging His position as one of those who do so joyfully or as those who do so in shame and defeat.

WE WILL SHARE IN HIS JOY

One more thing I would point out. On that inauguration day believers will share in His joy. Charles Spurgeon said it well,

> I have no doubt that every common soldier who stood by the side of the Duke of Wellington felt honored when the commander was applauded for the victory, for, said he, "I helped him, I assisted him; it was but a minor part that I played; I only held my position; I only returned the enemy's fire; but now the victory is gained, I feel an honor in it, for I helped, in some degree, to gain it." So the Christian, when he sees his Lord exalted, says, "It is the Captain that is exalted, and in his exaltation all his soldiers share. Have I not stood by his side? Little was the work I did, and poor the strength which I possessed to serve him, but still I aided in the labor;" and the commonest soldier in the spiritual ranks feels that he himself is in some degree exalted when he reads this [3]

This isn't hard to understand. When we stand on the sidelines of a game and cheer for our team we share in the joy of the team's victory. Everyone talks about how "we" won. They walk a little taller and feel a sense of satisfaction and pride. And yet, we made no key blocks. We had no great tackles, runs, or pass receptions. We didn't make a basket or get the big hit. In fact, we aren't even on the team. We cheered from the sidelines . . . yet we shared in the joy.

Try to imagine what a great day that Heavenly inauguration will be? The more involved we are with Christ now, the greater will be the joy on that day. It will be unlike the joy of a sports championship. The position of champion is temporary. Within a few months that championship must be earned again. But imagine the satisfaction that will come in Heaven to know that the battles are over. This is no temporary victory. . . it is final. It is complete. There will be no challenges . . . ever.

PRACTICALLY SPEAKING

In light of this future heavenly inauguration what difference should these facts make in our daily living NOW?

First, we need to make sure that we are on the right side. We will not get to Heaven by merely learning the right words. We must trust the Savior. So you and I have to search our hearts. Is our faith superficial or is it real? Does the Savior know us? Do we have a relationship with Him or only a passing contact? Are we really trusting Christ for our salvation or are we hoping that we can produce the right formula, or learn the right words, or do the right deeds? If our hope is in our own efforts we are on the wrong side.

Second, we will reflect Christ's Lordship in Our Priorities. If we know that Jesus Christ is Lord and someday everyone will acknowledge this, it seems to only make sense that we would honor Him as Lord in our day-to-day living. Let me be direct and to the point. Do you acknowledge Christ as Lord in your day to day living? Are you obeying His commands, fighting his battles, and maintaining loyalty to His purposes? Are you willing to honor His Lordship and seek His will for your life decisions? Are you willing to serve Him in ways that may not always be convenient? How important is Jesus to you?

Finally, we will relax. I remember the good old days when the Chicago Bulls were a perennial Championship team. Each spring I watched the NBA playoffs. During the course of each playoff game my emotions would swing from despair to elation as the lead changed hands. Life is like that a good portion of the time. We have great times and we have deeply trying and discouraging times.

I purchased a number of the highlight films from those years . . . and do you know what? When I watch them, I relive the excitement . . .but not the anxiety. What makes the difference? It's simple: I know they are going to win! And that's what makes our life different . . . we can live confidently because we know that Christ will one day sit on the throne and reign supreme. Life is filled with struggle . . . but the child of God knows the outcome.

The battle is won. Salvation has been purchased through the blood of Christ. When we trust Him . . . our future is certain. We no longer need to fret about Heaven . . . instead we can begin preparing for it. We don't need to keep looking over our shoulder; we can concentrate on looking ahead. The victory is certain.

Life won't always be easy. We won't always understand what is going on. Sometimes we will need to remind each other that the ending is already written . . . the campaign is over. The transition has begun. And some day, there will be a celebration that will last for all eternity. And in this knowledge there is good reason to be joyful.

Discussion Questions

1. What has been the greatest celebration you have ever participated in? Compare that celebration with the celebration that Paul points to in Philippians 2:9-11.
2. Do you agree with the statement that we spend a good portion of our time trying to claim the position that rightfully belongs to Christ? How would you defend your position? Give some practical examples.
3. Why does Jesus deserve to be exalted?
4. Some religions proclaim that Jesus is Lord, but they also say someday we will all be gods and lords of our own worlds (at least everyone who is part of their religion). How is their view of Jesus different from the view of Paul in Philippians 2?
5. How should this knowledge of a coming inauguration help lead us to joy?

7

Working Toward Joy

Philippians 2:12-13

I believe the Bible is a practical book. It gives us instruction that can benefit us in life. In fact, I believe this so strongly that I had some fun teaching my congregation to look for application in their study.

In many churches the congregation and the speaker have a familiar litany. The speaker says, "And all God's people said . . . " and the people respond "Amen." Well, I changed that . . . just a little. I told our congregation that we needed to apply Christian truth. Therefore every time I said, "And all God's people said . . . " I wanted them to respond, "So What?" (A few people decided to have some fun with me and responded, "who cares?")

At various points in my message you would hear this litany,

"And all God's people said. . . "

"So what?"

"I'm glad you asked"

Then I would proceed to give some applications for the points I was making. (It was interesting once at a community worship service when the speaker said, "And all God's people said . . . !")

In 2 Timothy 3:16, 17 Paul tells us that, *"All Scripture is God-*

breathed and is useful for teaching, rebuking, correcting and training in righteousness, so that the man of God may be thoroughly
equipped for every good work." The Bible is *useful* to *equip* us for
living. Any preaching or teaching that is not practical is teaching
that has missed the mark.

There is a great deal of doctrine in the Bible but that doctrine is
always leading us to a practical purpose. We are instructed in the
truth so that it can guide us in our living.

In the first eleven verses of Philippians 2 Paul wrote doctrinally
(and we saw plenty of practical application) and beginning with
verse 12 (through the remainder of the letter) the apostle Paul gets
very practical. He has laid the foundation and now gives us the "So
what?"

> Therefore, my dear friends, as you have always
> obeyed—not only in my presence, but now much
> more in my absence—continue to work out your
> salvation with fear and trembling, for it is God who
> works in you to will and to act according to his good
> purpose. (Phil. 2:12,13)

In these two verses Paul gives us several practical instructions.

Work Out Your Salvation

The first command given by Paul is that we should "work out
our salvation". There is a great deal of misunderstanding and confusion attached to these words. Paul does not tell us to work FOR our
salvation. He is not saying we must work hard to gain or earn (or
even keep) our salvation. Such an idea would contradict the rest of
what Paul has taught (go back to chapter one). Such an understanding negates the entire foundation of grace that has been laid down
for us.

People often feel that they must produce BEFORE they can be
"saved". They believe they must live a little better, learn a little
more, suffer a little longer, and be a little more religious before they
can know the forgiveness offered in Christ. In other words, they
believe they must earn God's grace!

The Bible tells us that we are forgiven and made new because
Christ paid for our sin on the cross, not because *we* paid for our sin.

Paul reminds us in the book of Romans that something that we receive in response to what we do, is not a gift; it is a wage. Salvation is a gift from God.

We don't work FOR salvation; but we are to work OUT our salvation. Paul is encouraging us to give expression to our salvation in the way we live. We are to APPLY our salvation to our living. I can think of several things involved in working out our salvation.

- We are to work at making sure that our hope is truly grounded in Christ and not on our own efforts
- We are to work at taking advantage of the ways that God has given us to help us grow. We should read the Bible, pray, worship, serve, give, meditate, fast and many of the other disciplines he has given us for growth.
- We should work to make a break with sin. We are not to just sit back passively, but must work at repentance and renewal.
- We are to work at adopting and applying the positive behaviors that the Bible admonishes. In other words we are to work at cultivating love, compassion, kindness, generosity, faithfulness, endurance as well as other qualities.
- We are to guard against the influence of the world by adjusting our friendships, amusements, and our use of time in order to combat the real presence of sin in our lives.

Working out our salvation means that we are to live on the basis of what is true in our lives and heart. We must tap into the strength that God gives us through His Spirit.

Do So With Focus and Determination

We are told that we are to do this work with "fear and trembling". In other words we should pursue this work with a holy vigilance and circumspection. It means that as I work out my salvation, I should realize the tremendous seriousness of what I am doing."[4]

Living the Christian life is not a leisure activity. Living as a child of God is something that should impact every element of our living. Following Christ is the most serious endeavor that we are about.

This is serious work for several reasons. <u>First</u>, we are in a battle.

We know that we are fighting a formidable foe in the Devil. Of all the terrorist threats we may face, the most dangerous terrorist is Satan and his army. He has access to the most vulnerable parts of our soul. His resources are considerable, and his weapons are massive.

We must be serious, because he is serious. Peter tells us "Your enemy the devil prowls around like a roaring lion looking for someone to devour." (1 Pet 5:8). Paul told us to "put on the full armor of God so that you can take your stand against the devil's schemes. For our struggle is not against flesh and blood, but against the rulers, against the authorities, against the powers of this dark world and against the spiritual forces of evil in the heavenly realms." (Eph. 6:10-11). The Devil is taking this contest seriously, and we had better take it seriously as well.

Second, we should be serious because we know our own weakness. We know that we are prone to be hot one minute and cold the next. One minute we are all excited about serving the Lord and the next we are indifferent. We know that if we don't keep after ourselves we will drift away. We are constantly in danger of becoming lukewarm, or compromising the faith. We work at our salvation because we know that if we don't, we will begin to drift.

Third, we should be serious in our desire to grow because we respect the Lord's discipline. Children often do the right things at first because they know if they don't, there will be consequences to pay. The Bible is clear; because the Lord loves us, He also disciplines us when we drift away. He is committed to our growth. He will move us toward growth one way or another. And I don't know about you, but I have discovered that avoiding the Lord's discipline is always a good idea.

Fourth, we should be serious about the work of discipleship because we know that God is serious about our relationship with Him. He took it seriously enough to send Christ to die so that our relationship with Him would be possible. When we treat discipleship as a joke, we make light of the Savior's love.

Finally we should be serious because of the benefit to be gained. The reason to get serious about physical exercise is because of the benefit that is received. Exercise allows you to have more energy, know greater health, and be more productive. I don't like to exercise most of the time, but I do like the results that the exercise brings.

Paul wrote to Timothy, "...*train yourself to be godly. For physical training is of some value, but godliness has value for all things, holding promise for both the present life and the life to come.* (2 Timothy 4:7,8). People make time for physical exercise because they know it is important to their health. Training in godliness is even more important. What will benefit us more than a close relationship with the Lord? Who does not want that "peace that passes all understanding"? Who wouldn't love to reach their family and friends with the good news of the gospel? To receive the benefits you need to be diligent in the work.

Do So Consistently

Paul acknowledged that the people in the church in Philippi worked hard at growing in faith while he ministering to them. He encourages them now to be continue to be faithful in his absence. We should live consistently for Christ whether others are watching or not. Integrity in the faith is something that is revealed in the hidden times more than in the public times.

> It is not what we eat
> but what we digest
> that makes us strong;
> not what we gain
> but what we save
> that make us rich;
> not what we read
> but what we remember
> that makes us learned;
> and not what we profess
> but what we practice
> that makes us Christians.

— Author unknown

Someone has said, "integrity is who you are when no one is

looking." It a the reminder that *who we are when no one is looking* is who we really are. We can all maintain a certain image when we are in church but the real test of faith is the person we are outside of the church. The goal of the Christian is to live consistently. Will Rogers summed it up well, "Live in such a way that you would not be ashamed to sell your parrot to the town gossip."

Paul would urge contemporary Christians to be consistent in our faith

- in worship
- when out with our friends
- when we are alone on a business trip
- when flipping through channels at night
- when on a date
- when pursuing amusements
- when we do something wrong
- when we are aggravated
- when we are on the Internet late at night
- when we are filling out tax forms
- when we are out with a potential client

Living the Christian life is a full-time pursuit. Paul urges us to pursue a God-honoring life in every aspect of our living.

Remember to Give God Credit

After being told we are to work hard at bringing our faith into everyday life it would be easy to despair. When we consider our weakness and inconsistency we might feel that we can never succeed. Thankfully, Paul follows his challenge to diligence with these wonderful words: "it is God who works in you to act according to his good purpose."

Paul proclaims God will give us the desire and the determination to do what we should be doing. Frankly, there are some people who are very uncomfortable with this verse. They say God is violating our "free will". Dr. Boice helps us understand this whole idea of a free will.

> You have free will to decide certain things, but you
> do not have free will to decide all things. You can

decide whether you will go to work on Monday
morning or pretend you are sick. You can order
turkey over roast beef at a restaurant. But you cannot
exercise your free will in anything that involves your
physical, intellectual or spiritual capabilities. By
your own free will you cannot decide that you are
going to have a 50 percent higher I.Q. than you do or
that you will have a gift of dealing with quantum
mechanics. You do not have free will to make a
billion dollars. You do not have free will to run the
100-yard dash in eight seconds.[5]

We are not able to follow Christ by our own strength. It is
against our nature. When Adam and Eve sinned, all their descen-
dants lost the capacity to be holy. And over time we lost our capacity to even truly love God. Paul says there is "no one righteous, not
even one; there is no one who understands; no one who seeks God."
(Romans 3 10,11)

As we have seen, the Bible teaches that even the faith we exercise is something that God has first planted in us. He is working in
us to get us to will (desire) and do (practice) according to His good
purpose. Do you realize how important and valuable this is? This
means several important things

- God understands our weakness and is more committed to
  helping us than we are committed to helping ourselves.
- We are not left to simply work to muster more of our strength
  but we are invited to tap into His
- We don't have to worry about falling away in the end because
  God is working on our desires and appetites so that we won't
  want to drift away.
- The victories and accomplishments we have in the spiritual
  realm should be acknowledged as coming from the Lord . . .
  and we should give Him the glory.
- We CAN live the Christian life.

Practically Speaking

Paul reminds us that the Christian life is a combination of right belief and renewed living. God is not primarily concerned that we know enough to pass a theology exam. Theology (a right understanding of God) is important, but God wants more. He is concerned to make us into new people.

When we come to the Savior we must come realizing that the process of salvation is something God begins and God brings to fruition. But it is also a process that requires our work . . . our diligent and persistent work. The two go together.

We must make a conscious effort to build our spiritual life. We need to cooperate with God's Spirit. We need to build it into our schedule, put it in our budget, and nurture it in our heart. Here are some specific ideas,

- Set a goal of reading through a Christian book every couple of months
- Replace the secular music with Christian music
- Find a Bible reading plan that will give you daily exposure to God's Word and then use the same time every day for reading and meditating on God's truth
- Make plans to get involved or start a Bible Study
- Keep a spiritual diary where you record what God is teaching you each day
- Find some Christian friends who will encourage you regularly and hold you accountable
- Memorize Scripture
- Work to make worship an attitude rather than a ritual. Pursue God more than you pursue getting a good feeling or obtaining new insights.
- Look for new opportunities to serve
- Get into the conscious habit of giving God credit for the things He does in and through you

Does this sound like work? I won't kid you; it *is* work. It is a task you will work on for the rest of your life. At times it will be very difficult. At other times it will be wonderfully delightful. But please know that the stakes are very high. This is not a hobby or an amusement. Our faith in Christ is not something we can separate from our daily living. It is to be our life's pursuit to grow in the

Lord. It is not easy but we are not left to do this on our own. The Lord will be with you equipping you and cheering you on, every step of the way.

Discussion Questions

1. Do you understand the distinction between working OUT your salvation and working FOR your salvation? Why is this *Rely on God for strength* distinction important? *So we don't miss God's grace & truth*
2. How does this working out of salvation contribute to our pursuit of joy?
3. Do you know someone who is working very hard to EARN grace? Do you know any who have misunderstood grace and feel they can do as they please because God will forgive them? What would you say to each of these people to help them find the true way?
4. Why is consistency important in the Christian life?
5. What discipline(s) has been helpful to you in your Christian walk? Talk to others and share what you have learned about working out your salvation.

8

Living as Stars in the Night

Philippians 2:14-18

I'm not much of an outdoorsman (I do mow the lawn), so I am not really "in tune" to nature like some people are. But one of the things I love about living in rural America is the ability to gaze at the stars at night without the glare of streetlights and the obstruction of urban "haze".

As I look at the Heavens I can't help feeling better about life. The stars remind me that I am part of a giant universe. The splendor of those stars reminds me that there is a Creator who is wise, powerful, and knows my name.

The joy-filled believer is like a star in the blackness of the world. The true Christ-follower is not only one who is internally joyful . . . they also reflect joy to those around them. Jesus said,

> *You are the light of the world. A city on a hill cannot be hidden. Neither do people light a lamp and put it under a bowl. Instead they put it on its stand, and it gives light to everyone in the house. In the same way, let your light shine before men, that they may see your good deeds and praise your Father in heaven.*
> Matthew 5:14-16

Someone said, Christians are to be more like thermostats than thermometers. A thermometer reflects the temperature; a thermostat sets the temperature. Christians are to influence behavior rather than simply parrot the behavior of the culture in which they reside.

Not long ago I was backing out of a parking spot in my vehicle. I felt the transmission slip (it didn't quite engage). I noticed the problem but didn't think much about it until it happened again. I stopped by the mechanic and asked him to look at it. It turned out that this little thing was not so little. There was a seal in the transmission that had cracked. If I had continued to drive the vehicle disregarding these little things I might have found myself on a highway someplace stranded because the vehicle would not shift gears.

Let me give you a little quiz. Is putting oil in your car occasionally a minor thing, or a major thing? Is remembering to take your blood pressure medicine a little thing or a big thing? Is remembering to pay your taxes a little thing or a big thing? Is forgetting your wife's birthday a minor thing or a major thing?

In this chapter we will look at a bunch of seemingly little things. But these little things can turn into big things if we don't address them. They will siphon joy from our life and diminish our reflection of the Savior in a dark and dreary world.

> *Do everything without complaining or arguing, so that you may become blameless and pure, children of God without fault in a crooked and depraved generation, in which you shine like stars in the universe as you hold out the word of life—in order that I may boast on the day of Christ that I did not run or labor for nothing. But even if I am being poured out like a drink offering on the sacrifice and service coming from your faith, I am glad and rejoice with all of you. So you too should be glad and rejoice with me.* (Phil. 2:14-18)

Don't Complain

The word translated complaining or grumbling is an onomatopoetic word. What that means is that the Greek word, *gongusmos* sounds like what it is describing. Go ahead, say it out loud! "Gongusmos". It sounds like a grumbler doesn't it?

We see grumbling all around us. We grumble about employers, coaches, teachers, spouses, pastors, and of course, politicians. We grumble about the weather, about the price of merchandise, about our churches, about the lighting in restaurants, and at times, we even grumble about how God runs the universe.

We are guilty of grumbling when we find ourselves whispering in corners. We are grumbling when we complain and when we whine. The grumbling person always sees the negative side of everything. They are the people who live by some of Murphy's Laws

- Nothing is as easy as it looks; everything takes longer than you think; if anything can go wrong it will
- The other line always moves faster
- The chance of bread falling with the peanut butter-and-jelly side down is directly proportional to the cost of the carpet.
- Inside every large problem is a series of small problems struggling to get out.
- 90% of everything is crud
- Whatever hits the fan will not be evenly distributed
- No matter how long or hard you shop for an item, after you've bought it, it will be on sale somewhere cheaper.
- Any tool dropped while repairing a car will roll underneath to the exact center.
- The repairman will never have seen a model quite like yours before.

Grumbling people are unhappy people. It is impossible to be joyful and be a person who is always grumbling. A grumbler always feels like they are being cheated. They highlight the negative traits in others and they are always ready for a fight. Grumblers seem to feel better when they can complain about others. They aren't happy and everyone around them knows they aren't happy.

Let's be honest, grumbling people are annoying to be around. These folks have the marvelous ability to suck the life out of any party. After you talk to a grumbling person for very long you are exhausted. A complainer can "infect" everyone around them.

Nothing is ever good enough for a complainer. They always know better. They will never know the sweet satisfaction of contentment.

A complainer is like a cancer; everywhere they go they destroy life. These people like to play the part of a martyr. They feel that no one likes them. And for the most part, they're right.

A Grumbling person is at heart a person who resists what God has given. God wants us to receive all His gifts with trust and joy. The complainer doesn't do this.

In Numbers 14 the Israelites sent spies into the land God had promised to the Israelites. These twelve spies came back with their report. They talked about what a good and fertile land it was. And then they began to grumble. They said the people were too big and strong. They concluded that it was impossible for them to take the land.

God was fed up with the complaining. Since the people didn't have the faith to trust Him and instead chose to complain, God decided that He would condemn these people to die in the wilderness. You may not know this, but the reason the Israelites wandered for 40 years in the desert was because they chose to grumble rather than believe.

In 1 Corinthians 10 Paul points to this same occasion and writes,

> *And do not grumble, as some of them did—and were killed by the destroying angel. These things happened to them as examples and were written down as warnings for us, on whom the fulfillment of the ages has come. So, if you think you are standing firm, be careful that you don't fall! No temptation has seized you except what is common to man. And God is faithful; he will not let you be tempted beyond what you can bear. But when you are tempted, he will also provide a way out so that you can stand up under it. Therefore, my dear friends, flee from idolatry.* 1 Corinthians 10:10-14

I find it interesting that Paul talked about learning a lesson from the grumbling of the Israelites, and followed with the command, "flee from idolatry". This is not coincidence. Grumbling is a sign that we trust our analysis of things rather than trusting God. In our times of grumbling we are insisting that we know what we need better than He does. In other words, we are playing God. The Bible calls that idolatry.

Don't Argue

Paul also says we should not argue. The word for arguing is the word *dialogismos*. It's the same word from which we get our word dialog. There are two parts of this command.

First, we are not to argue with each other. You and I both know not much can be accomplished in an argument. Tempers flare, good judgment disappears, and no one listens. Unfortunately, many people have turned away from the gospel because they got tired of watching Christians fight.

We have an argumentative spirit if we find ourselves attacking another rather than seeking solutions. We have this spirit if we immediately defend ourselves before we hear what another is saying. We are argumentative if we raise our voice (an attempt to shout down the other.)

Do some people like to argue? I think some people do. As a boy I used to enjoy arguing with an umpire, any umpire. I remember one time arguing with a youth leader at a youth rally. I argued that an answer to a Bible trivia question was wrong and I did it in quite an animated fashion. (By the way, I was wrong). I was always look-ing for an argument to become involved in. It made me feel impor-tant, significant, and powerful but it made me look like a fool.

I've known people who try to pick apart anything someone says. They are ready for an argument. You get the feeling that all you have to do is open the door and all kinds of venom will come spew-ing out. You see this regularly on talk shows. A host visits with an audience just waiting for that innocent person to say the wrong thing so they can have a fight on their hands.

I don't like watching arguments. I don't like listening to argu-ments (is there anything worse than visiting someone's home and finding yourself in the midst of a argument between the host and hostess?). I don't even like arguing any more. Arguing is not productive. Arguments leave winners and losers. Friendships are destroyed not strengthened.

We need to learn from Jesus. He chose to remain silent when accused rather than give his opponents cause for action. We would be very wise to adopt the posture of silence as well. It is better to be mistreated than to turn people away from the gospel of truth. It is better to listen than to fight.

Second, and more importantly we are not to argue with God. We argue with God more than we are willing to admit. We question His ways, we resist His commands, we say we want to "discuss things" with the Almighty. Any time we do this, we take a step away from trust and a step toward rebellion.

It is certainly acceptable for us to express our confusion and our frustration with the things of life. There is nothing wrong with being honest about our feelings with the Lord. However, when we begin to attack God's wisdom, we cross a line. As God said to Job, "Who are you to question the Almighty".

We are to avoid complaining and arguing. To state it positively we are called to be encouraging, positive, affirming, loving and trusting.

The difficult condition

These commands are tough enough but Paul adds another word that seems to make obedience impossible. He tells us we are to do *everything* without complaining or arguing. Let that sink in for a minute. There are lots of things we can do without complaining and arguing . . . but everything? That is like saying that you have to give up all sweets. You may have no trouble giving up many of the sweets but ALL of them?

I was wondering how taking this command seriously would impact our lives.

- What would it mean for doing our chores?
- How would it change the way we watched an extracurricular activity at the school?
- How would it impact how we respond to interruptions?
- How would it change our discussions about politics?
- What difference would it make to the way we get out of bed

in the morning?
- How would it change our conversation about other Christians and churches?
- How would it change the way we handle differences of opinion?
- What would happen to gossip?

Paul doesn't give us any loopholes here. He says we are to put grumbling and arguing away. Instead we are to be positive, calm, and trusting people. But what is really surprising is the reason he gives us for this.

The Rationale
In the text Paul follows his commands with the words "so that". It means that Paul is now listing for us the motivation for a living a positive, trusting life instead of a grumbling, contentious life. Paul gives us the pay off for working at our conversation. Listen to the text,

> **so that** *you may become blameless and pure, children of God without fault in a crooked and depraved generation, in which you shine like stars in the universe as you hold out the word of life—in order that I may boast on the day of Christ that I did not run or labor for nothing.*

I see three reasons in these verses for eliminating complaining and contention from our lives. <u>The first reason is eliminating these things from our life is essential to spiritual growth.</u> Do you hear that? You cannot become blameless, pure, or without fault as long as you continue to complain! Ouch!

These words encourage us to live in such a way that others will have no reason to blame us or accuse us. We are to be pure, which means we are to be blameless not only externally, but also in our heart. We are to be people who harbor no ill will, provoke no conflict, and engage in no backbiting or slander. We are to live like Jesus, whose opponents could find nothing against Him.

This is impossible to do if we are constantly grumbling about others, our circumstances, and the "raw deal" we have in life. If we want to be blameless, pure and without fault in the way we live, we will have to develop a different attitude and learn to speak differently. James understood this. He wrote, "*If anyone is never at fault in what he says, he is a perfect man, able to keep his whole body in check.*" Jas. 3:2

So you tell me, "Is this a little thing or a big thing?" Our attitude and demeanor has a big impact on our spiritual maturity.

<u>Second when we don't grumble or argue we become a beacon in a dark and dreary world</u>. We live in a world that is crooked and depraved. It is a place where truth is distorted. All you have to do is look around and flip through the channels on television to know that this analysis of the world is certainly true. But let's not whine about society (remember, we aren't to grumble!). Hear Paul's point. When we act with a cheerful and trusting attitude we will bring light to the darkness. We will stand in stark contrast to those around us.

Consider a lighthouse on a seacoast. A lighthouse is placed on a dangerous coast to warn vessels of peril and to save them from shipwreck. In the same way a Christ-honored life shines in a dark world and helps people to find their way to the Father.

Many people leave the church and Christianity because of a conflict situation in their church. But it is also true that many are drawn to Christ because of the loving people they meet. In the early church the people on the outside may not have understood the gospel, but what they did understand was that the Christians loved each other. People were drawn to these people because of the light that shined bright.

This shouldn't be as unique as it seems to be, but those who are positive, encouraging, loving, patient, and willing to suffer rather than strike out, will stick out in the world. People notice those folks and want to know what make them "tick". Those people are like a magnet . . . people are drawn to them.

Every time you and I get sucked into one of those conversations where we sit around and criticize everyone, we proclaim to the world that we are no different than they are. Our witness is diminished and our light dims.

Paul gives one final reason for living this way,

in order that I may boast on the day of Christ that I did not run or labor for nothing. But even if I am being poured out like a drink offering on the sacrifice and service coming from your faith, I am glad and rejoice with all of you. So you too should be glad and rejoice with me. (v.16-19)

Paul says when we obey these commands we not only stand as light in the world, you make others proud. Paul was a Pastor and I can really understand his heart here. When I see growth in my congregation it makes me feel like my labor has been directed well. When I see them excel in matters of faith I share in their success. I understand what Paul is saying.

But you also understand if you are a parent. If you have ever watched your child excel you know that there is a sense of pride that you feel also. When you see your children mature into responsible adults your feel like you must have done something right as a parent. When they receive an award or honor you feel like you are receiving it as well. I think this is what Paul is saying. When our words are joyful, enthusiastic and careful we show that our teachers did well.

When we live consistent, God-honoring lives others are encouraged. Other believers draw strength from our example and they are spurred on in their faith. When a believer stands confidently in the time of trial, others are encouraged to stand as well. When a believer holds their tongue, others are encouraged to do likewise.

I love Eugene Peterson's rendering of this passage,

Do everything readily and cheerfully—no bickering, no second-guessing allowed! Go out into the world uncorrupted, a breath of fresh air in this squalid and polluted society. Provide people with a glimpse of good living and of the living God. Carry the light-giving Message into the night so I'll have good cause to be proud of you on the day that Christ returns. You'll be living proof that I didn't go to all this work for nothing.[6]

PRACTICALLY SPEAKING

O.K., so now it is time for the rubber to hit the road. I think it is sometimes helpful to take warnings and turn them into positive statements. So, if we look at this text backwards here's what we have: if you want to bring joy to the Father, if you want to bring joy to those who have taught you, if you want to shine like a lighthouse on a storm-tossed sea, and if you want to be a sensible voice in a confused world, the way to begin is to stop grumbling and arguing!

Our attitude toward our daily life and our attitude toward each other apparently has a great impact on the world in which we live. Our willingness to trust God rather than debate with God apparently is more important than we realized.

So, what do we do? How do we begin the process of change? Probably we should start by recognizing that we need to make some changes. I speak as a fellow struggler who has on occasion enjoyed a "pity party" or two. My family would tell you that I am one of the best whiners in the world. So here are some suggestions for you and also for me.

- When you get up in the morning try saying, "Good morning, Lord!" rather than "Oh No"
- When you start to argue with God learn to say, "Lord, I don't understand . . .help me to trust you."
- Ask someone to make a grumbling sound (perhaps *gongusmus*) every time they hear you complaining or arguing. Ask them to help you become aware of the problem. It's annoying but effective.
- Look for productive ways to deal with problems rather than standing around and criticizing
- Avoid gossip
- Keep a flashlight, lighter or picture of a starry night in a prominent place and use it to remind you that you are to shine like the stars in a crooked and depraved world.
- Remind yourself that your attitude is a choice.

It all sounds so simple doesn't it? And yet you and I know it is not as easy as it sounds. Every time we resolve to change our attitude, Satan will be determined to point us to the negative. For every advance we make, Satan will remind us of every failure. I wish we could just snap our fingers and change our attitude, but we can't. But God can help us change. He can help us see people instead of opponents; opportunities rather than burdens; joy instead of drudgery; grace rather than bondage; hope rather than despair. He can help us trust rather than fret; wait rather than panic; and believe rather than fight.

And while God is doing all these things inside of us, He will help the world see light instead of darkness and truth instead of error. And He will do that through you. So the question that remains is this: do you want to be a thermostat or a thermometer?

Discussion Questions

1. How do you respond to those who complain and argue? Do you fight back? Do you walk away? Do you avoid these people? What do you think is the correct response to someone who complains and argues?
2. Are "most" Christians thermometers or thermostats?
3. Do you see yourself as a complainer? If not, in what kinds of circumstances are you most likely to complain?
4. Why do some people seem to delight in arguing? When should you fight and when should you refrain from fighting? Be careful, look for principles that you can apply to all circumstances.
5. Of the suggestions listed, which do you think you can use? What additional suggestions might you add to the list?

List — Reminder of light.
Attitude is choice.

9

Savoring The Blessings of Friendship

Philippians 2:19-30

Each week I meet with a group of ten to twelve men at 5:30 a.m. for 45 minutes of Bible Study and prayer before the workday. To be honest, my list of fun things to do has never included getting up before the sun. My alarm goes off at 4:20 a.m. so I can have the coffee ready by 5:00 a.m. Every week when that alarm goes off I can't believe I am getting up in the middle of the night! However, I have found that even though my body rebels at the thought of getting up this early, my spirit is eager. I'm eager to get going because it is a chance for me to be with some of the people in my life who I call my friends.

Over the years this group of men has met together and prayed together though many heartaches and joys. We know we aren't perfect. We try to be honest about our struggles. We try to be "there" when times of testing and trial come. That's what friends do.

People talk rather glibly about friendship. But if you have a good friend, you know what a treasure that person is. The Bible understands this as well. Whenever the Bible speaks about friendship, it does so with great seriousness. We are told to choose our friends wisely because ties with the wrong friends lead to trouble. We are told that friendship is one of the richest treasures of life. Solomon understood the value of friendship. Listen to some of the things he wrote,

> *A friend loves at all times, and a brother is born for adversity.* Proverbs 17:17

> *Wounds from a friend can be trusted, but an enemy multiplies kisses.* Proverbs 27:6

> *As iron sharpens iron, so one man sharpens another.* Proverbs 27:17 (NIV)

> *If one falls down, his friend can help him up. But pity the man who falls and has no one to help him up! Also, if two lie down together, they will keep warm. But how can one keep warm alone? Though one may be overpowered, two can defend them- selves. A cord of three strands is not quickly broken.* (Ecclesiastes. 4:10-12)

Solomon affirmed the importance and the value of friendship. Henry Brooks Adams wrote, "One friend in a life is much, two are many, three are hardly possible." Finding a good friend is difficult, and it seems to be more difficult all the time. There are many things that hinder our desire for close friendships
- The pace of life . . . we are too busy to nurture relationships
- The distractions of life . . . television, the Internet, video games
- The mobility of life . . .people move frequently from job to job and location to location
- The isolation of life . . .we spend much time at computers and in front of boxes which provide no interaction at all.
- The cynicism of life . . . we distrust people and so we are reluctant to let our guard down

All of these things serve as barriers to true and lasting friend-ships. In this chapter we will learn some things about the joy of friendship from some of the personal comments of the Apostle Paul in Philippians 2:19-30 (NIV)

> *I hope in the Lord Jesus to send Timothy to you soon, that I also may be cheered when I receive news about you. I have no one else like him, who takes a genuine interest in your welfare. For everyone looks out for his own interests, not those of Jesus Christ. But you know that Timothy has proved himself, because as a son with his father he has served with me in the work of the gospel. I hope, therefore, to send him as soon as I see how things go with me. And I am confident in the Lord that I myself will come soon.*

> *But I think it is necessary to send back to you Epaphroditus, my brother, fellow worker and fellow soldier, who is also your messenger, whom you sent to take care of my needs. For he longs for all of you and is distressed because you heard he was ill. Indeed he was ill, and almost died. But God had mercy on him, and not on him only but also on me, to spare me sorrow upon sorrow. Therefore I am all the more eager to send him, so that when you see him again you may be glad and I may have less anxiety. Welcome him in the Lord with great joy, and honor men like him, because he almost died for the work of Christ, risking his life to make up for the help you could not give me.*

In these words Paul describes two of his friends, Timothy and Epaphroditus.

Timothy was a young man Paul helped lead to a saving relation-ship with Christ. His mother and Grandmother were Jewish believ-ers but his father was a Greek. After Timothy became a believer he became Paul's loyal companion. He was with Paul when he minis-tered in the cities of Philippi, Thessalonica, Berea, Corinth,

Ephesus, and he was with him in prison in Rome. Timothy was associated with Paul in the writing of no fewer than five of his letters—1 and 2 Thessalonians, 2 Corinthians, Colossians and Philippians; and when Paul wrote to Rome, Timothy joined with him in sending greetings. Paul trained Timothy for the ministry personally. The letters of 1 & 2 Timothy were addressed to this dear friend and companion.

Epaphroditus is a man we know little about. We only read about him in the letter to the Philippians. Apparently, Epaphroditus was sent by the church in Philippi to help care for the Apostle Paul. While Epaphroditus was with Paul he became seriously ill. His illness must have lasted for a long period because the Philippians heard about it and had sent word back about their concern for Epaphroditus (which involved a long period of travel). We have no way of knowing what was wrong with Epaphroditus. We are only told that Paul was concerned about him.

Paul uses some strong words to describe this man. He calls him, "my brother, fellow worker and fellow soldier, who is also your messenger, whom you sent to take care of my needs." (2:25) Such strong words lead us to believe that a strong bond had been created between the men.

If we look closely at both of these men we see at least three qualities of a good friend.

PRESENCE

The first characteristic of friendship in Timothy and Epaphroditus is that they were there with Paul. Remember, Paul is not on a speaking tour. He is in jail. There was a good chance that the Emperor Nero was going to have Paul executed. It was also a distinct possibility that those who were "known associates" would also be at risk. Consequently, we aren't surprised that many people kept their distance.

We forget that Paul's job was one that would leave him pretty lonely. He traveled much and had many demands on his time. Paul had lots of people around him . . .but I suspect few knew him well. When Paul was popular, lots of people thought of themselves as Paul's friend. But when Paul was in trouble, those "friends" disappeared. In 2 Timothy 4 Paul wrote to his dear friend Timothy near the end of his life. Paul confesses his loneliness and asks Timothy to come and be with him.

This is why the idea of presence is so important to friendship. Friends are the people who are there when others are not. When the crowd dies down after a crisis, your friends are the ones who are still active and involved. Friends will,

- Sit with you in a hospital
- Sit quietly as you grieve
- Be available at a moment's notice in a crisis
- Come out to help in the middle of the night
- Lend a hand when there is work to be done
- Listen happily when there is a joy to share
- They will still be there when everyone else has grown tired of your pain and sorrow.

When others could not, or would not travel to be with Paul, Timothy and Epaphroditus were by his side. These two men were dear to Paul because they were at his side helping in the work of the gospel and helping him personally.

As you probably know, Jackie Robinson was the first African American to play major league baseball. While breaking baseball's "color barrier," he faced jeering crowds in every stadium. While playing one day in his home stadium in Brooklyn, he committed an error. His own fans began to ridicule him. He stood at second base, humiliated, while the fans jeered.

During this time, the shortstop, "Pee Wee" Reese, came over and stood next to him. He put his arm around Jackie Robinson and faced the crowd. The fans grew quiet. Robinson later said that arm around his shoulder saved his career.

Do you think that Pee Wee Reese received some criticism for what he did? Of course he did. At that time in our history I would bet that Pee Wee Reese even received death threats because of his actions. It didn't matter. Reese was not going to allow a friend and a teammate to face that kind of persecution alone. Timothy and Epaphroditus would not allow their friend to be left alone either.

Do you have this kind of friend? If so, thank God for them.

Maybe a more important question is, "Are you this kind of friend to anyone?" A friend doesn't have to have profound words or great ability . . . they just need to be there.

SACRIFICE

A second characteristic of friendship in both Timothy and Epaphroditus was their willingness to sacrifice.

They Gave of Themselves

Paul says of Timothy,

> *But you know that Timothy has proved himself, because as a son with his father he has served with me in the work of the gospel. I hope, therefore, to send him as soon as I see how things go with me. And I am confident in the Lord that I myself will come soon.* (22-24)

Paul called Epaphroditus a "fellow worker". He served beside Paul.

Timothy volunteered to take this letter to the church in Philippi when no one else was willing to do the job. It meant time away from home (remember it would take many weeks to travel to Philippi in these days). It meant inconvenience. And it also meant travel, which at times could be quite dangerous. Epaphroditus came to Paul; Timothy was willing to serve Paul by going to the Philippians.

A friend will do what they can to help another. They will give their time, their resources, and their energy. A friend is not afraid to get involved with your life. They are willing to roll up their sleeves and help.

They gave with no thought of themselves

Paul says about Epaphroditus,

> *Welcome him in the Lord with great joy, and honor men like him, because he almost died for the work of Christ, risking his life to make up for the help you could not give me.*

The word for "risked his life" is a gambler's word and means to stake everything on a turn of the dice. Paul is saying that for the sake of Jesus Christ and in order to assist Paul, Epaphroditus gambled his life.

Do you see what Timothy and Epaphroditus had in common? Of Epaphroditus we read, "[he] takes a genuine interest in your welfare. For everyone looks out for his own interests, not those of Jesus Christ." You can't be a good friend if you are only looking out for your own interests. Friendship is not about you . . . it's about your relationship to and with your friend. Sometimes friendship is inconvenient. Sometimes it is unpopular. Sometimes it is difficult. But if you only desire friends who will say nice things to you and never demand anything in return, you will never have a close friend.

These men were not looking out for their needs. They weren't with Paul out of some warped desire to gain notoriety. They weren't concerned about what happened to them. They were serving the Lord first and in their service to the Lord, they served Paul. They gave their time, their substance, and their energy.

The story goes that two friends were fighting side by side on the battlefield. The combat was fierce and many men were dying. One of the friends was wounded and couldn't get back to the trenches. The other friend went out to get him, going against orders from his superior. He returned with his friend who was dead and in the process had become mortally wounded himself.

The officer looked at the dying soldier and said, "It wasn't worth it."

The soldier replied, "O but it was sir. When I reached my friend, he looked at me and said, 'I knew you'd come.'

You don't get *true* friends because of the car your drive or the money you have. Don't get me wrong, you can get people to hang out with you because of what you have, what you look like, the influence you hold, or because of what you do . . . but when somebody has something better, those friends will be gone. A solid friendship is built on relationship, not superficial things. A good friend is not there because of what they can get from you. They are there because of what you mean to them. They will gladly give of themselves for you.

Jesus said, "Greater love has no man than this, that a man would lay down his life for his friends."

ENDURANCE

There is one more characteristic, these men were not only friends for a short period of time; they were friends for the duration. Timothy traveled with Paul. He was there when he was in jail and when he neared the end of his life. Timothy was still there to carry on the work of his dear friend after he was gone.

We've alluded to it several times, but it must be stated clearly: A good friend is one who is with you for the long haul. A friend understands that everyone makes mistakes and at times we all do stupid things. So, they don't desert you when you do something foolish. They don't walk away because you had a bad day. They don't become scarce because times are rough. They hang in there. They are committed.

My dad is suffering from Alzheimer's disease. It is difficult to be my dad's friend right now. His disease has made it tough to talk with him and going places with my dad is a stressful experience because he will sometimes do socially embarrassing things. You can't reason with him and at times the situation can be quite exasperating.

My parents have found that many of their friends are now staying very far away. And we understand. It's hard. But they do have a few friends that have been there for them throughout the experience. My parents have found out who their best friends are. One of these friends has been dad's friend since they were kids.

They don't live close but they visit often. They will spend the night with my parents and invite mom and dad to come and spend some time with them. They go out to eat even though it is difficult. This friend takes my dad out golfing because it is something he enjoys. They work to make time for my parents even though it is difficult. They don't stay away. And when they are around, dad's day is brighter and mom's is easier. They are good friends.

Some of you have had good friends like that. When times were tough you were not surprised when your friend stood by you . . . even though it was unpopular. Perhaps they put their arm around you like Pee Wee Reese, or maybe they provided for some special needs. Maybe they sat by your bedside in the hospital or visited you in jail. And maybe they were the one who was leading the cheers for your accomplishments.

Former televangelist Jim Bakker was convicted of fraud and deceptive practices. His conviction was a major embarrassment for the church. The news media had a field-day with the charges and cover-up. Bakker went to prison, lost his ministry, lost his wife, and did some deep soul searching.

In his book, *I WAS WRONG* Bakker mourned the fact that many of those he thought were his friends deserted him. The one grand exception was the Billy Graham family. They visited him in prison and when he was released they provided a home for him to live in. They invited him to church. That first Sunday when Jim Bakker went to church he was seated with the Graham family, right next to Ruth Graham! The Grahams made a bold statement that day. Jim Bakker was their friend and they didn't care who knew it.

Everyone would have understood if the Grahams kept their distance from Jim Bakker. Association with this man might tarnish the reputation of this respected family. But shunning Bakker was not an option for them because Jim Bakker was their friend. He had made mistakes. He had had hard times . . . but true friendship is not fickle.

Practically Speaking

Paul didn't set out to teach us about friendship. But the Holy Spirit teaches us through his words nonetheless. Let me share some final thoughts.

First, <u>everyone needs a friend.</u> We all need someone we know we can depend on. I think every one of us recognizes that true friends are hard to come by. If you have one of these good friends, take some time today to thank God for this person and make it a point to say to them, "I'm glad you are my friend." Let them know how much you appreciate what they mean to you.

Second, recognize that <u>in order to have good friends we need to be a good friend.</u> If we want friends, we can't wait for people to come to us. We can't wait for people to show that the love we extend will be reciprocated. Our job is to be friendly. We must give of ourselves to others. Some people will take advantage of our love. But some won't. Some will use us, but some people will become our friends. You and I must make the first move. We must be friendly and somewhere along the line, God will help us find the friends we are looking for.

Third, we must be patient. Friendships do not develop over night. They develop over time. Be friendly with many and over time you will discover who your real friends are. In fact, it may surprise you who your real friends turn out to be. They will be the ones who stand with you in the tough times, who share your joy as well as your sorrow and they will be the people you cherish for the rest of your life.

Finally, the best way to learn about friendship is to be a good disciple. Have you noticed that being involved, giving of yourself, and being committed for the long haul are also the traits that are called for in following Christ? These men grew as friends because of their common love for and service to our Lord.

This leads me to conclude that some of the best friendships we have will be found in the community of faith. They will often be found among the people you worship with on a regular basis. As we serve the Lord, we will grow together. As we follow the example of Christ, we will find ourselves becoming better friends. As we learn more about His commitment to us, we will find ourselves more willing to be committed to each other. And as we do this, I think we may be able to show the world that friendship is made stronger, when we are one in Christ.

May God lead you to develop and cherish those special relationships that bring strength to your life and joy to your heart. . . .even if you have to get up at 4:20 a.m. to find them.

Discussion Questions
1. How would you define a true friend? Do you have any of these friends? Describe the process of growing to be friends.
2. Do you think it is true that we are fortunate to have one true friend and supremely blessed to have more than that? Why do you think so, or why don't you think so?
3. Do you think it is easier to have friends in the city or in the

country? Why?

4. Of the three characteristics of a true friend; presence, sacrifice, and endurance, which do you think is the most difficult and rare?

5. If you were to sit down with your child to talk to them about making friends, what would you tell them?

1. A friend cares for you. Encourages you. Stands up for you. Sad when your sad, Happy when your happy. Will tell you lovingly if you are making a mistake. Listens.

Process - Time - Experiences life together - Sharing common bonds

2. Yes.

3. - In the Christian Community it is easier.

4. Endurance may be more difficult

5. Go to places to meet - Get to know people - Be kind - invite potential friends to home or to go places. Talk, Listen, enjoy getting to know people. Work together on meaningful projects. Help to reach Goals.

Other friend of Paul - (Phillipians)

Barnabas - Encourager

? Mark

Personality Type

"Harmonizer"

Need to be present

10

Overcoming the Barriers to Joy

Philippians 3:2-11

I have a very vivid memory from my days in Elementary School. I attended Chicago Public Schools and when I was in eighth grade I was made the captain of the safety patrol. (The safety patrol was a group of students who would stand at busy intersections and "guard" students who needed to cross the street). It was really quite prestigious at the time.

As captain of the patrol boys my job was to make sure that all the corners were covered and everything was running smoothly. One day I was walking to check on one area of the patrol boys. My path took me past a home that had a little dog in the backyard. The dog was noisy but I didn't pay it much attention. Every time I walked by this house the dog barked. On this day however as I walked by the house suddenly from out of the bushes this deranged, vicious, and I suspected rabid, miniature poodle came at me with it's teeth exposed. (O.K. I know the idea of being scared of a poodle seems absurd but *you* weren't there.) I was a terrified. I began running and I think I may have been screaming (or whimpering).

The owner of this vicious monster either saw or heard what was going on and called the dog back to its home. I avoided that home from then on.

With this particular history in mind you can understand why I am particularly attentive when the Apostle Paul tells us to beware of dangerous dogs. The dogs Paul refers to are not poodles, but teachers who pervert the gospel. These teachers were leading people astray and keeping the Philippians from knowing the joy that God wants us to know and experience. The particular teachers Paul addressed were known as the Judaizers.

The Judaizers were a group of people who said they believed that Jesus was the Savior . . . but only the Savior of the Jews. Therefore the only way you could become a Christian was to first become a Jew. You had to convert to Judaism, be circumcised, and conform to all the Jewish rituals and laws.

This was a big controversy in Paul's day. And though we don't have Judaizers around today, there are others who do much the same things that the Judaizers did. They sound good. They seem religious. But they are really wild dogs attacking the foundation of the true gospel. If we aren't careful, they will siphon the joy from our lives.

Paul writes,

> *Watch out for those dogs, those men who do evil, those mutilators of the flesh. For it is we who are the circumcision, we who worship by the Spirit of God, who glory in Christ Jesus, and who put no confidence in the flesh* [Philippians 3:2-3]

In this chapter we are going to erect some "Beware of Dog" signs. We want to become alert to the things that can steal joy from our lives and hearts.

Beware of Those Who Focus on Religious Performance

Paul calls the Judaizers "mutilators of the flesh". He is referring to their emphasis on circumcision. It is not that the act of circumcision itself was bad. Circumcision was an act established by God in the time of Abraham as a special sign to each Jewish male that they (and their seed) were in a unique and special relationship to God due to God's promise on their behalf. The rite of circumcision has a good purpose.

Paul's objection was the teaching of the Judaizers that said a Gentile (uncircumcised person) could not become a believer unless they first went through this Jewish rite. They made circumcision a pre-condition to salvation.

Paul argues (especially in Galatians) that any pre-condition of salvation implies that there are certain things we must do in order to qualify or deserve salvation. These pre-conditions take the focus off of God's gracious act on our behalf and put it instead on things that we can do for ourselves. This perverts the gospel message.

Paul labored to point out that we are saved by what *God* has done for us. We are helpless. We must depend totally on His promise and grace or we have not understood either the nature of our sin (which is greater than we can undo), the nature of our ability (our sinful tendency perverts even the good acts we try to do), or the scope of God's grace.

Let me sharpen our focus a little. These "dogs" still exist today. We still want to require people to conform to our standards and opinions. The heresy of the Judaizers lives on. When you least expect it one of these vicious distortions of the gospel will attack. We may not require that people be circumcised to be a "true believer" but we are often confronted with demands such as,

- You must be baptized in a certain manner in order to be saved
- You must have a certain kind of conversion experience. (You might have to repeat certain prayers, walk forward at a meeting or have a particular experience like speaking in tongues)
- You need to read from a certain version of the Bible
- You must give up certain behaviors before you can be saved (you must not smoke, drink or chew or go with girls who do)
- You must abide by the accepted dress code
- You can't be a genuine believer unless you worship on Saturday rather than Sunday

There is a good chance that some of the things in this list you laughed off as being absurd. But there may have been something in the list that made you defensive. If something made you defensive that may be the performance that you have placed before grace. Please think long and hard about these issues.

Any time we make something other than genuine repentance and personal reliance on Christ as a requirement for salvation, we are making salvation a matter of grace plus works and robbing the Savior of the glory that is rightfully His! And every time we establish a pre-condition to salvation we set up barriers that may keep people from the Savior. Every time we allow something as a pre-condition to salvation we poke a hole in the reservoir of joy.

Beware of Those Who Emphasize Personal Accomplishment

There is a second but related barrier to joy and it is an emphasis on personal accomplishments. The joyful Christian does not put confidence in their experience, their education, their memberships or their service. They put their confidence in Christ! Listen to Paul,

> *If anyone else thinks he has reasons to put confidence in the flesh, I have more: circumcised on the eighth day, of the people of Israel, of the tribe of Benjamin, a Hebrew of Hebrews; in regard to the law, a Pharisee; as for zeal, persecuting the church; as for legalistic righteousness, faultless. But whatever was to my profit I now consider loss for the sake of Christ. What is more, I consider everything a loss compared to the surpassing greatness of knowing Christ Jesus my Lord, for whose sake I have lost all things. (4-9)*

Let me suggest a contemporary paraphrase of Paul's words,

> I was a church member all my life. I took lots of classes and received a theology degree with honors. Everyone agreed that I was a model Christian. I served on boards and committees and aggressively defended the faith. I was baptized as an infant and an adult. I was "sprinkled" and "immersed". I took communion as often as it was offered and I always gave more than my tithe. Christians of all denominations admired me.

Paul looked good. The thing that kept Paul from the Lord was not his sin . . . it was his goodness! He didn't respond to Christ, because he thought he was doing pretty well by himself! In fact, the majority of people around us are hoping to "get to heaven" because they think they are good enough. They are trusting in their achievements, accomplishments and goodness.

Do an informal survey sometime. With a group of friends (it may be eye-opening to do this at a church gathering) ask, "Do you think you will go to Heaven when you die?" And then follow up with the question, "Why?". I think what you will find is that people will respond with answers such as this:

>"I hope so . . . I think I've lived a good life"
>
>"I try to live by the Ten Commandments and the golden rule"
>
>"I think I live better than most people"
>
>"I think I have done my best"
>
>" I doubt it, I've made a lot of mistakes in my life"

The common thread in each of these responses is that the focus is on "I" rather than "God". Each person is looking to their own goodness (or lack thereof) as the basis of their salvation. They trust their "track record" rather than the work of Christ.

The key verse in this passage is verse nine. **The true gospel is "being found in Christ, not having a righteousness of my own that comes from the law, but that which is through faith in Christ — the righteousness that comes from God and is by faith."** (Philippians 3:9)

Righteousness is a word that means right standing. To be in right standing with God, we have to have met God's requirements. Unfortunately for us, God's requirement for salvation is perfect obedience. We cannot meet this standard. We cannot . . . in our own strength do what is required for salvation. The message of the gospel is that Christ provided the perfect righteousness we need and paid for the sin we committed. Our sin was transferred to His account. His goodness was applied to our account. Because of Him we are righteous. He provides the good in the transaction . . . we provided the bad. Our performance, our so-called "good deeds" add nothing. Salvation is ALL of Christ. He alone gets the glory. We put NO CONFIDENCE in the works of our flesh. We rely 100% on Christ and 0% on our own efforts.

Someone came to a Orthodox priest one day and asked, "Father, Are we saved by faith or by works?" The answer was filled with wisdom. "Neither. We are saved by God's mercy." You see, even when we talk about faith we sometimes make it something that we need to "muster". Faith is not a "work" we produce to be saved. We don't have to "muster" faith. Saving faith is a belief or a trust that what God has done in Christ is enough.

D. James Kennedy has a good illustration,

> Imagine you are standing on the brink of a cliff. Across the chasm 200 feet away, is another cliff. The distance to the bottom: 5000 feet. You have to get across the chasm to get to the other side. You have a strong nylon rope that is capable of holding 3,000 pounds without breaking. It will easily support you — but it's only 100 feet long. You are 100 feet short of bridging the 200-foot gap.

> Here I come to your rescue. "Don't worry," I say, "I was a Boy Scout. I'm always prepared. Here's a spool of thread — more than 100 feet long. We can tie my thread to your rope and you'll have no trouble getting across."

> Would you trust your life to my spool of thread? Why not? It's very good thread. Oh, I see — you don't think it's strong enough to support you.

> Well, let's change the scenario a bit. Let's say that instead of 100 feet of strong rope, you have 190 feet of rope. Now you only have to rely on my thread for ten of the 200 feet. You can cross the chasm now, can't you? No? You mean you still don't feel safe to cross?

> Okay, let's change the scenario once again. Instead of 190 feet of rope you have 199 feet, 11 inches of good, stout rope. Now, there's only *one little inch* of thread in that entire span. Surely you can

trust it now. Surely you can make the crossing of the chasm in complete confidence. No! Well, why not?

Because rope plus thread cannot save you! It must be good, stout rope all the way across or it cannot support you. And it is the same story with faith and works. Only faith in Christ is strong enough to support you. Faith plus works cannot save you. Your salvation cannot be 50 percent Christ and 50 percent you. It can't be 60/40 or 75/25 or even 99.99/.01. Christ must be your entire support, your entire salvation. [7]

Does it feel like I am beating this point to death? I'm sorry if it seems that way. But this is *essential* Christianity. You MUST get this point. And Christians must constantly be on guard lest we forget this tenet of faith.

WAYS TO GUARD AGAINST THE JOY-ROBBERS
See Yourself Clearly

Paul confesses that he "considers everything a loss compared to the surpassing greatness of knowing Christ Jesus my Lord." (Philippians 3:8) The word "consider" shows us that Paul has made a choice to refuse to rest or point to his actions as a reason for his salvation. He is constantly reminding himself that he is just an "old sinner saved by grace."

When we remind ourselves of our sinfulness, several things happen. First, we become open to genuine worship. We can't worship when our focus is on our methods, devices, and ability. Genuine worship takes place when our focus is the majesty and grace of our loving Father, demonstrated through His Son, and brought to our hearts by His Spirit.

Second, when we see ourselves clearly we will have a greater experience of salvation. We will no longer carry the burden of trying to save ourselves. When we understand and receive God's grace totally apart from our works, our confidence is in Him. We no longer have to "perform" and we can be honest and genuine before Him. As a result, we will know the incredible freedom (and joy) that comes from forgiveness.

Third, we will be a better witness for the Lord. Instead of confusing people with our requirements, we will be pointing them to Jesus. Instead of trying to change people ourselves, we will introduce them to the one who brings real change in a life. Instead of adding barriers to those seeking God, we will remove the barriers.

Seek to Know Christ and More

Paul says, "*I want to know Christ and the power of his resurrection and the fellowship of sharing in his sufferings, becoming like him in his death, and so, somehow, to attain to the resurrection from the dead.*" (Philippians 3:10)

The best way to defend yourself against the dogs of faulty theology is to be well acquainted with what is true. Paul's passion was to know Christ better. The better He knew Jesus, the less susceptible he would be to those who would distort His words and claims.

In today's world we would say that this was Paul's purpose statement. He wanted to know Christ better. What is wiser than seeking to be close to the One who knows the way to joy and happiness? What is smarter than drawing close to the One who knows the best course for your life to take? What makes more sense than walking with the One who has the strength to help you survive any storm? What could be more delightful than getting to know the One who has loved you since the creation of the world?

We (and I include myself) spend a good deal of time distracted from the truly important things of life. Management guru Steven Covey has made a living by encouraging people to live their lives based on the important things and not just by the urgent things. We need to hear that message. If we really want to know joy we must move our Christianity from the back burner of our life to the front burner. Christ must be the hub of our life and not just one of the spokes.

Paul says he is motivated and captivated by a desire *to know the power of Christ's resurrection*. Perhaps Paul is saying that he is looking forward to the day when he will be free of his sinful and worn body. Maybe he is looking forward to the life that is to come.

But it also may be that Paul is yearning to experience the practical difference the resurrection makes to life right now. He wants to know that sense of victory that comes when the fear of death is removed. He wants to know the freedom, the joy, and the sense of confidence that is anchored in Christ's resurrection. He doesn't want to wait till heaven . . . He wants that power to impact and change Him now!

Third, Paul says he wants to know the *fellowship of sharing in His sufferings*, becoming like him in his death. I'm betting that you have never even thought about adding such a statement to your own personal mission statement. Who would want to share in His suffering? We spend most of our life trying to avoid suffering. We take pills, have surgeries, and even (if we are honest) compromise our beliefs in order to avoid suffering.

Paul is not saying that he wants to suffer. Nobody *wants* to suffer. Paul however understands that following Christ will inevitably bring some suffering. Obedience is costly. If we stand with Christ (as we should) we will be standing against the world.

Paul's desire is to receive and to react to the sufferings of this world in the same manner that Jesus did. Paul wants to face the trials of life not as a threat, but as an opportunity to grow and testify of the Savior's goodness and love. He wants to have that same confidence in God that Christ had.

And finally, Paul says he hopes to "somehow, *to attain to the resurrection from the dead.*" At first reading, this sounds like it contradicts everything Paul said earlier. It sounds like Paul is telling us that he is hoping that he can *make it* to heaven. He is hoping that he will be good enough, remain diligent enough, to actually get into Heaven. But that is not what he is saying. Paul has no doubt about his eternal destiny. He is the one who told us in chapter one, "he who began the good work in us will bring it about to completion." He is the same one who told us in Romans, "nothing will separate us from the love of God." Paul's confidence is in Christ and Christ alone.

Dr. Boice points out that the Greek word for resurrection here literally means to "place" or "stand up". In the Greek world, living people were seen as standing up while dead people were lying down. Boice suggests that Paul is saying that he wants to be a person who is standing up in a world where everyone is lying down.

He wants to show others that he is living a new life in a dark and dreary world.

Of course it is also possible that Paul is merely speaking with humility. Paul seeks to know Christ, to experience the power of the resurrection, and to face suffering with the perspective and faith of Christ. And after all of this, he knows that it is still by God's mercy and grace that he will know the joy of eternal life.

Do you see where the apostle's heart is here? This should be our goal as well. Rather than spend all our time running around trying to be "good enough", we should spend our time trying to know, enjoy, and follow the one who has made our redemption possible. And if we were to do this, several things would be true,

- We would focus more on our relationship with God than our activity for God
- We would know peace rather than anxiety
- We would be bold rather than timid
- We would risk more and fear failure less
- We would know joy even in times of crisis
- We would offer grace to others without first demanding that they "be like us"
- We would spend the rest of our lives marveling at His mercy and grace

Practically Speaking

There are three things I hope you take away from this chapter. First, it is my prayer that you realize Jesus doesn't want your list of good deeds. He wants your heart. And let's be frank, sometimes the hardest thing to do is to admit that you can do nothing to help yourself. It's tough to accept a true gift. But that's what salvation is . . . accepting Christ's sacrifice as payment for your sin.

If you have spent your life concerned that you might not be good enough for Heaven, let me put your mind at ease. You are NOT good enough for Heaven. And neither am I. Salvation is a gift. Instead of trying to earn God's grace, receive it.

Second, perhaps you are a Christian but you feel burdened by "all you have to do for the Lord". I hope you will realize that it is not about what you can do for the Lord. It is about what He can do in and through you. Having come to the Father by grace, we must remember to walk in that grace. Our job is to act as He commands and then step back and watch what He can do. We don't have to change the world . . . we just need to let Him change us.

Third, I hope that a reminder of what we have received will challenge you to live life gratefully. I pray for a new focus to your worship and a new humility in your heart. I hope you will be moved to know Christ not simply in an intellectual sense but in a fresh and practical way and that you will strive to apply the reality of the resurrection to your daily living. I hope you become a person who is standing up in a world that is filled with spiritually dead people. If we live this way we will not only know an uncommon joy . . . we will be able to keep the dogs on a leash where they belong.

Discussion Questions

1. What place do you think theology plays in the practical experience of joy?
2. Based on this chapter, what would you say to the person who says, "Why do you think you are going to Heaven?"
3. In what ways do we set up barriers to joy? Be specific. What teachings, what rules, what understandings lead us into slavery rather than to joyful freedom in Christ? What does your church teach is necessary for salvation?
4. What place does baptism, communion, obedience, tithing, experience have in the life of the Christian?
5. What do you think it means to "share in the sufferings of Christ"?

11

Striving for the Best

Philippians 3:12-14

One of the things that plagued me in my efforts to excel in school was the curse of the "good enough". When it came time to write a paper for English or one of my Bible classes I often quit when I believed the paper was "good enough". (Now, in fairness I should point out that we didn't have computers or word-processors when I was in school. I also wasn't a good typist. Re-writing a document was a lot more work than it is today. Look at that, I'm still making excuses!) When I studied for a history, psychology or philosophy test I often reviewed only until I thought I had done a "good enough" job to "get by".

A person who settles for the "good enough" (I confess with shame) is a person who is settling for second best. They are content to coast with the crowd rather than push on to excellence. You can see this plague in many area: education, competitive sports, personal training, parenting, management of our finances, making household repairs, cleaning our vehicles . . . and in our spiritual life.

Let's be honest, when it comes to our Christianity, most of us are happy to remain in the mainstream. We are happy to have a "good enough" faith. If we are spending daily time with God, worshipping regularly, and serving in some capacity in our church, we feel satisfied. We are equal to or ahead of most people we know so we figure we are "good enough".

That was not the attitude of the Apostle Paul. Listen to what he said,

> *Not that I have already obtained all this, or have already been made perfect, but I press on to take hold of that for which Christ Jesus took hold of me. Brothers, I do not consider myself yet to have taken hold of it. But one thing I do: Forgetting what is behind and straining toward what is ahead, I press on toward the goal to win the prize for which God has called me heavenward in Christ Jesus.* [Philippians 3:12-14]

Paul refused to settle for second best. Here was a guy who was known throughout the Roman Empire (and this without television or radio). He was a chief figure in the Christian Church and the first true theologian. He was a popular pastor and conference speaker. He was an established author. Most of us would feel this was "good enough". We would be quite satisfied with such achievements. But not the Apostle Paul.

Paul refused to rest on his achievements. He was not seeking earthly "success" but a heavenly reward. He wanted to live faithfully and to glorify God with every breathe of his life. Paul's desire was to lead everyone to the knowledge of the saving grace and power found in Jesus Christ. Every joy-motivated believer must refuse to settle for "good enough" as well.

In this chapter we are going to look at Paul's prescription for combating spiritual complacency. It's so simple; it's profound.

WE MUST REALIZE GOD HAS A GOAL FOR OUR LIFE

Paul says, "*I press on to take hold of that for which Christ Jesus took hold of me.*" The words I want you to see are the words, "that for which Christ Jesus took hold of me." Paul understood that the Lord took hold of his life with a goal in mind. And this is true for all of us.

Romans 8:28 is a verse many know by heart. Verse 29 is less

known. Paul writes, *"And we know that in all things God works for the good of those who love him, who have been called according to his purpose. For those God foreknew he also predestined to be conformed to the likeness of his Son, that he might be the firstborn among many brothers."* Do you see God's purpose in calling us? He wants us to be conformed to the likeness of his Son.

God's desire is that we grow to be like Christ. God's goal is not just to "get us in the door". He is not looking to merely "save us", He wants to "transform us". A Christian is one who is ever moving toward Christ-like-ness. We should be making progress toward holiness.

Please understand that God has a job for you to do. He has called us TO something. We are a part of His plan. God DOES have a plan for your life. His plan will lead you to joy, fulfillment, contentment and eternal blessing.

RECOGNIZE THAT YOU HAVE NOT ARRIVED YET

Paul not only recognizes that the Lord had a grand purpose for his life, He realized that he had not arrived at that purpose yet. Paul knew that he was not what he should be. He was aware of his faults and the areas where he still needed to grow. The word for "perfect" can also be translated "complete". Paul recognized that he was not finished yet.

Please hear this. Some people get discouraged because they feel they aren't progressing very rapidly. They seem to feel that they should have "arrived". Paul shows us that the life of walking with Christ is a life of growth and maturity . . . much like life itself. Growth takes time. As diligently as Paul worked at his faith, he still had not arrived. Don't get discouraged . . . keep moving forward. Growth takes time.

We must measure ourselves by Christ. He wants us to be pure in our actions, in our conversations, in our thinking, in our attitudes, in our relationships. He wants us to love Him more than anything else. He wants to be in the position of influence in every part of our life. If you understand the standard, you will, like Paul, realize that there is still work to be done.

DON'T LIVE IN THE PAST
What this doesn't mean

Paul tells us that if we want to be focused on our growth we must "forget the past". Obviously Paul is not telling us to literally not remember anything (although as I get older I'm finding it easier and easier to forget). We should (and must) remember who we were before Christ found us. We should remember the many times when we have seen God's faithfulness demonstrated. And we also need to remember the mistakes we've made so that we can avoid them in the future.

Paul is not telling us that we don't have to fulfill the responsibilities of the past. If we have wronged someone, we should try to make it right. If we have stolen from some one, we should make restitution. If we have a problem with someone, we should seek to be reconciled. Paul is not telling us to forget these things.

What it does mean

When Paul tells us to forget the past he is saying we can't and must not live in the past. What happened in the past is past and we must keep going forward. There are two reasons we need to forget the past. First, we have a tendency to <u>fixate on the past</u>. We hold on to some bad experience and it becomes an anchor that weighs us down. We remember a hurt that someone inflicted and it eats us up. If we don't forget a time when we stumbled we will determine to never try again. How we deal with the painful times of the past will determine how we live in the present. We must learn from the pain and then move on. What God has forgiven should never be taken as a burden again.

Second, we have a tendency to <u>rest on the past.</u> We will replay the past victories and be content to remember instead of continuing to push ahead. This happens to many people. There are Christians who are always talking about the great times of faith in the past. They talk about how intimate their relationship with Christ WAS.

These people (and I do it on occasion too), will talk about the way they witnessed enthusiastically when they were in college, or sang in a group, or shared the gospel on street corners. If you were to ask them whom they have witnessed to lately, they have a hard time coming up with an answer.

There are many Christians who talk about the great growth that took place in their life when they were in a youth program, or went to camp, or when they enrolled in a Bible correspondence class. But if you ask them what new insights they have gained recently, they can only shrug. They are resting on a past experience!

Sports teams have this problem. They have a great victory and then glow from that victory . . . and in the next game they lose to an inferior opponent because they lost their focus. The same is true even in preaching. I usually allow myself Sunday and Monday to enjoy or learn from a worship experience. But by Monday afternoon I have to focus on the next week. I have found that I must keep looking forward and not backwards.

BE INTENTIONAL ABOUT YOUR GROWTH

Paul tells us that he "presses on". This is the same word that was used in verse 6 when Paul talked about his zealous persecution of the early church. It is with that same kind of intensity that Paul pursues God's plan for his life. Paul tells us "this one thing I do". He is single-minded. Paul was not distracted. He was clear where he was headed.

Paul was stretching forward and reaching for his goal. He is not only concentrating, he is straining forward. The image is that of running in a race. You have seen people near the finish line leaning forward to try to beat their opponent to the tape. This is the image Paul uses for his desire to grow spiritually.

Some of mankind's greatest contributions have come from people who decided that no sacrifice was too large and no effort too great to accomplish what they set out to do. Edward Gibbon spent 26 years writing The History of the Decline and Fall of the Roman Empire. Noah Webster worked diligently for 36 years to bring into print the first edition of his dictionary. It is said that the Roman orator Cicero practiced before friends every day for 30 years in order to perfect his public speaking. Read the stories of the great preachers of years past. They preached every day! Many of these men spoke in many different places every week but unlike today, they didn't just preach the same message to different audiences.

Men like Calvin, Wesley, Luther, Lloyd-Jones, Spurgeon have volumes of sermons that they preached over the years. What stamina! What persistence!

Now contrast these examples with how much energy we put into the Lord's work. The comparison can be rather embarrassing. It should lead us to ask ourselves some heart-searching questions: Why is our service for Christ sometimes performed in a halfhearted manner? Why do other things always come before our time with the Lord? Why do we prepare more diligently for our responsibilities in the world than we do our responsibilities in the church?

Growth will not happen if we are haphazard about our spiritual life. Practically diligence means,

- making time for God in our schedule
- finding time to thoughtfully read the Bible
- planning for times of prayer
- establishing worship and service as a priority in our calendars
- doing a regular and honest spiritual evaluation of our lives
- pushing ourselves to study and read for growth
- diligently preparing for our teaching opportunities
- daring to reach beyond what is always comfortable and safe

Paul wanted God's best in his life and was unwilling to stop until he reached that goal. On the contrary we have a tendency to stop not long after we have left the starting blocks!

KEEP YOUR EYE ON THE GOAL

Paul tells us that he always keeps his eye on the prize. It is like the Olympic athlete who trains tirelessly for a gold medal at the Olympics. When they get tired they imagine what it will be like to stand on the platform and hear the National Anthem of their country being played. That picture spurs them on.

Years ago a young black child was growing up in Cleveland, in a home which he later described as "materially poor but spiritually rich."

One day a famous athlete, Charlie Paddock, came to his school to speak to the students. At the time Paddock was considered "the fastest human being alive." In his talk with the students he said, "Listen! What do you want to be? You name it and then believe that

God will help you be it." One little boy decided that he too wanted to be the fastest human being on earth.

The boy went to his track coach and told him of his new dream. His coach told him, "It's great to have a dream, but to attain your dream you must build a ladder to it. Here is the ladder to your dreams. The first rung is determination! And the second rung is dedication! The third rung is discipline! And the fourth rung is attitude!"

The result of all that motivation is that he went on to win four gold medals in the 1936 Berlin Olympics. He won the 100 meter dash and broke the Olympic and world records for the 200 meter. His broad jump record lasted for twenty-four years. His name? Jesse Owens.[8]

That is the kind of focus and determination we need. We may not have the motivation of a cheering crowd, a gold medal, and a national anthem. But there are some images that can motivate us. Think about what it would be like to

- stand before the Father and hear "Well Done!"
- have your life reviewed without any sense of regret or shame
- be surrounded by those who's lives have been redeemed partially because of your faithful witness
- have someone willing to testify that you were consistent and faithful during your funeral service
- have adults tell you about what a difference your Sunday School class made in their life when they were children
- bury a loved one knowing that they are in Heaven because you were there the day they made a commitment to Christ.
- see the joyful and proud eyes of Jesus that first morning in Heaven

These are the pictures that keep me going. I hope they spur you on as well.

Practically Speaking
For the Church

What does this message mean practically for the church? I think there are several good lessons.

- Though a congregation should be grateful for the growth and blessings they may have seen, they must always be looking for new opportunities to minister and grow.

- We must constantly evaluate our ministries and eliminate those that have served their purpose and develop those that meet the new needs around us.

- We must be on guard lest we value our traditions so much that they become an obstacle to growth. The question must always be, "Is this something that will further the Kingdom of God?" Rather than "Is this the way we have always done it?"

- We must remember that our goal is not a particular attendance figure, our goal is to honor and glorify Christ in all we do. When we pursue this goal we will surely see numerical growth, but the numbers are not our goal. Numbers are only a measurement tool. We can get numbers by giving stuff away. We could get numbers by providing good entertainment. But our real goal is not numbers . . . it is growth in Christ.

For Individuals

Many people begin a diet or start exercising and never follow through. Many start reading a book but never finish. Some begin a new course of study but give up when it becomes difficult. Others get married and get out when it becomes difficult. And there are some people who are fascinated by faith for a while and then grow bored and move on to something else that will excite them for a while. Are you like this? Do you have trouble finishing what you begin? Are you following through on your declaration of faith? Are you a temporary follower or are you committed to Christ?

The person who gives up misses out on the benefit that comes with hard work. The one who leaves a marriage misses out on a quality relationship. The one who gives up on exercise and diet sacrifices good health. Those who give up on education miss out on the insights they could gain. And those who give up the race for the heavenly prize miss out on the joy of walking with Christ.

I'm not trying to suggest that you do more things. Many believers are doing so many things that they are unable to do anything well. We are not called to greater activity. . . we are called to more focused living. In order to strive for excellence you may need to *eliminate* some of the things you are currently involved in so that you can give yourself fully to what God has called you to do. You may need to cut back so you can be more fruitful. Our goal is to reach the goal and not just to stay busy.

So, what is the one thing you are focused on? Paying bills? Gaining power? Having temporary peaks of enjoyment? Set your sights higher! Press for the prize! Refuse to settle for "good enough". Be a person who hungers for more of Christ. Refuse to rest on the laurels of the past. Live a vital present relationship with the Savior. Don't quit before the race is over.

Some of you are near the finish line. Your earthly life is nearing it's conclusion. Don't coast now! Now is the time to "kick" and to finish strong. Others of you are just getting started. Don't give up because it is difficult. Keep working . . . be patient. Growth takes time.

Perhaps you are right in the heat of the race. Don't let down. Keep pushing. I know it is exhausting at times. Focus on the goal . . . strive to finish well.

Paul encourages us to be more than names on a church roll. Paul wants us to have a vital, dynamic and growing relationship with the Lord. If you and I are going to heed his challenge then anything less than that dynamic, joyful, and growing relationship with the Savior will simply not be good enough.

Discussion Questions

1. In what specific ways do you think we are tempted to settle for "good enough"? (For example, when students take term papers off the Internet rather than doing the work themselves; or some Pastors do the same with sermons).
2. Why is the past both important and dangerous?
3. What is the difference between complacency and contentment? One is negative the other is positive. Struggle to understand that difference.
4. A Baseball manager might say to a professional team, "Our goal this year is to win 90 (of 162) games". If you asked Jesus what His goal for your life is, what do you think He would say?

5. What are some examples of "living in the past"?
6. Can you think of any practical disciplines that would help
   you to "push ahead" in your Christian life?

12

Models: Good and Bad

Philippians 3:15-19

When I first felt called into the ministry I dreamt of becoming a great speaker like Billy Graham (after all, our initials are the same!). As I watched Dr. Graham I found myself imitating the great preacher. I'd fold my Bible back and hold it over my head. I practiced saying, "The Bible says. . . " (with that hint of a southern accent which of course sounded ridiculous coming from a teen in Chicago). Billy Graham was one of my early models of what preaching should be.

I gave up trying to be the next Billy Graham but I did learn from the gifted evangelist. In fact, I have learned from many great models over the years. Chuck Swindoll taught me the importance of application in preaching. The Welch Pastor D. Martyn Lloyd Jones taught me the value of preaching the principles Scripture reveals and helped me to see the wealth of material that is often hidden in a Biblical text. R.C. Sproul taught me to think theologically and precisely (he also increased the size of my vocabulary). James Montgomery Boice taught me about clear and practical exposition. Max Lucado taught me about drawing pictures with words.

It is human nature to model our lives after the people we

admire. As kids we throw the ball in the back yard and imagine that we are our favorite athletes. Some people dress as their favorite models or television personalities. If you admire someone and hang around them long enough, you will begin to pick up some of their style and mannerisms. (Try talking to someone from the south for an extended period of time and see if you don't begin to develop a little southern drawl yourself!)

Role models are natural and good. But they can also be dangerous. The wrong role model can lead us in the wrong direction. Some people are led into drugs, crime and immoral behavior because of the people they choose as their role models.

In 1 Corinthians 15:33 Paul quotes a Greek poet when he said, *"Do not be deceived: Bad company corrupts good morals"* If you have bad models you will move in the wrong direction in your Christian life. Good models will help us live joyfully; bad models will inhibit our joy. Let's look first at the negative.

CHARACTERISTICS OF BAD MODELS

> *For, as I have often told you before and now say again even with tears, many live as enemies of the cross of Christ. Their destiny is destruction, their god is their stomach, and their glory is in their shame. Their mind is on earthly things.* (3:18,19)

I see five characteristics of poor role models in Paul's words,

Bad Models are enemies of the cross

Bad models are enemies of the cross because they diminish what Christ did on that cross. They preach a false way of salvation. They either minimize his work and emphasize our efforts (we call this legalism); or they use the cross as a license for sin. These people might say, "Since Christ has saved us, it doesn't matter how we live our lives. It doesn't matter what we do. We can sin all we want and still go to Heaven." (Theologians call this antinomianism.)

A bad model is always going to lead us away from resting in the grace of God. We talked about this in the chapter ten.

Bad Models are Ruled by their Appetites

Poor models let their appetites determine their values rather than the other way around. They justify the way they behave by telling you that it makes them happy, or it "feels right", or "it is satisfying" or "it works". In each of these cases the standard is not the objective truth of scripture, it is the subjective truth of their feelings. In each case God's will is subject to the whims of man rather than the other way around.

If you have ever tried to diet you know what it is like to be ruled by your appetite. Your intention is to eat sensibly and to cut out the junk food so you can maintain better health and be more productive in life. Your intentions are good until your stomach starts grumbling. Many people start a diet right after a big meal and give it up as soon as they get hungry again.

The same is true in the spiritual life of many. They talk about obeying and loving the Lord but as soon as a strong desire for something sinful comes on them, they give in. Let me give you some examples of those who are governed by their passions,

- Those who refrain from calling wrong behavior sin because they don't want to alienate anyone.
- Those who spend money they don't have for things they don't need (but they think they need them)
- Those who justify their immorality
- Those given to gluttony
- Those who are prone to laziness
- Those prone to fits of anger
- Those who are constantly jumping from church to church every couple of years because "their needs are not getting met."

People who are led by their appetites are inconsistent. They will swing from one extreme to another depending on their situation and their feelings at any given time. Lying may be wrong in one situation but acceptable in another. Deception may be condemned today and embraced tomorrow.

Our appetites must be subject to the truth of Scripture and not the other way around! We need an anchor that will serve as a reference point when our appetites begin to control us.

Let's be honest, every one of us gives in to our appetites on occasion. The key is that we don't want to model our lives after a person who is habitually governed by their appetites. They are unreliable guides, just like our feelings.

Bad Models are Proud of What They Should be Ashamed Of

In 1 Corinthians 5 Paul writes to the Corinthians,

> *It is actually reported that there is sexual immorality among you, and of a kind that does not occur even among pagans: A man has his father's wife. And you are proud! Shouldn't you rather have been filled with grief and have put out of your fellowship the man who did this?* (1 Corinthians 5:1-2)

In the Corinthian church there was a man that was committing adultery with his step-mother! Rather than the Corinthian church being horrified, they were proud of their tolerance and open-mindedness! Perhaps they were proud of the fact that they "didn't judge" these folks.

Sin is destructive to people who engage in it (it deadens their conscience and causes them to drift away from the Lord) and it is destructive to the people around it. Being proud of our sinful behavior is a sign of our depravity and not our maturity.

Don't think that this was a problem that was unique to Corinth. We see this kind of thing in the church today! Immorality is approved of because it is "just the way things are." Practicing homosexuals are ordained or married in the church because people "can't help" the way God made them. Ethically and theologically empty techniques are used to draw a crowd for "worship" and these things are celebrated as resourcefulness! We practice ethically questionable business techniques and call it business savvy.

Sad to say, we have seen this in the highest office in the United States. It was well known that former President Bill Clinton engaged in immoral and unethical behavior and yet his approval rating went up! People seemed to admire the man's ability to "get away with it." These are the kinds of bad models Paul is talking about. A person who celebrates evil will continue to plunge deeper into it. Their conscience will get more and more calloused. These people will lead those who follow them away from God.

Bad Models Focus on Earthly Things

Bad models are looking to the wrong ends. Their goals are skewed. They are concerned about how they can make a name for themselves, how they can amass material things, how they can be "better than others". They look to earthly applause rather than heavenly approval. They want present satisfaction rather than heavenly joy. They want to preserve this life at any cost . . . even the denial of faith. They are building a kingdom on earth rather than in Heaven.

Does this kind of thing happen to Christians? Of course it does. Power and influence is seductive. It is easy to begin manipulating situations and circumstances so we can get more power, more influence and more stuff.

Bad Models are Heading for Destruction

These bad models may seem to be having a good time. They are laughing. They look like they are enjoying themselves. The world may call them prosperous. But they are enjoying themselves because of their ignorance. They are heading to heartache. Jesus said, "What will it profit a man if he gains the whole world, but still loses his soul." Bad models haven't thought that far ahead.

GOOD MODELS

All of us who are mature should take such a view of things. And if on some point you think differently, that too God will make clear to you. Only let us live up to what we have already attained. Join with others in following my example, brothers, and take note of those who live according to the pattern we gave you. (Philippians 3:15-17)

They Hunger to Know Christ Better

The first thing that Paul says about the good models is that they have the same attitude that he has. At first, this sounds terribly

arrogant. But think about what Paul was telling us,
- He recognized that he was in the process of growth
- He was constantly in search of a more complete and vital relationship with Christ
- His focus was on God's grace not his goodness

A good model is one that desires a vital relationship with Christ in the present and is not content with past accomplishments. The kind of model we should look for is the one who is constantly striving to honor and serve the Lord in their lives. These people aren't just seeking more information . . .they want to know Jesus and honor Him with every breath of their life.

They have a Teachable Spirit
Paul tells the Philippians that if they don't agree with him, "the Lord will make it plain to them." When I first read this, I reacted negatively. As I grew up I found myself in the company of a good many liberal Pastors (by this I mean these were men who denied basic Christian truth like the deity of Christ, the literal resurrection of Jesus, and the need to be "born again"). On various occasions we would talk about theological issues. Often these men would smile, pat my head, and dismiss me with the words, "Oh, someday you'll understand." The implication was clear: someday, when I was more intelligent, I would see that they were correct and I was wrong. I hated that pious arrogance.

At first it may seem like this is what Paul is saying. But that's not what he is saying. Paul understood that we grow at different rates. He knew people needed time to understand what he had come to understand. Paul is confident that God will make His will clear.

I remember having a conversation with the prominent theologian John Gerstner. I had asked Dr. Gerstner about some theological issues that had really made an impact on me. I confessed that I was very frustrated that others in my congregation did not share my enthusiasm for these doctrines. In his wisdom, Dr. Gerstner reminded me that I had been studying and wrestling with these matters extensively for many years. He suggested that I needed to continue to proclaim the truth, and then give people time to reach the same conclusions that I had reached over time. It was good advice.

People grow at different rates. We all must be open to grow in our knowledge of God. The minute we believe we have "arrived" is the same minute we will stop growing.

Do you know that the greatest hindrance to finding God's will for our life is our unwillingness to learn God's will for our life? Hear that again . . .the greatest hindrance to finding God's will for our life, is our unwillingness to learn God's will for our lives. Many of us who struggle with what God wants us to do aren't really struggling with what God wants us to do but are instead struggling to figure out how to get God to approve of what WE want to do. If you want to know God's will for your life you have to be teachable. You need to be open and attentive.

A good model is someone who is always open to learn and grow. A coach or a teacher can tell you that desire and openness to instruction is not the same thing. A person can have all kinds of talent and enthusiasm but if they aren't willing to learn from someone else, they are severely limited in what they can become. The greatest musicians, the greatest athletes, the greatest business minds all have one thing in common . . . they are eager to learn anything that will help them improve. They ask questions. They listen. They are receptive.

These kinds of models are the ones who keep their heads when there are disagreements in the church. These people will not compromise on core beliefs but they also aren't willing to be dogmatic on issues that aren't core issues. They are willing for the Lord to "make it clear to them." These folks are open to honest correction and willing to learn from anyone who can teach them. Their ego does not hinder their growth.

They Act on What They Say They Believe

Paul said, "*Only let us live up to what we have already attained*". What simple wisdom this is! Rather than spend all our time arguing over our differences and debating about what we don't understand, how much better if we acted on what we DO understand?

In fact, let me take this a little further. Paul can tell the Philippians to follow his example because he has worked to live consistently. This is the kind of person you want for your model . . .the one who lives consistently with what they say they believe. Jesus gave us similar advice. In Matthew 7 when he warned of false teachers, he told us that we would recognize them "by their fruit". In other words, we could tell by the way they live their lives. Warren Wiersbe writes,

> In the summer of 1805 a number of Indian chiefs and warriors met in council at Buffalo Creek, New York, to hear a presentation of the Christian message by a Mr. Cram from the Boston Missionary Society. After the sermon a response was given by Red Jacket, one of the leading chiefs. Among other things, the chief said:
>
> Brother, you say that there is but one way to worship and serve the Great Spirit. If there is but one religion, why do you white people differ so much about it? Why don't you all agree, as you can all read the same book?
>
> Brother, we are told that you have been preaching to the white people in this place. These people are our neighbors. We are acquainted with them. We will wait a little while and see what effect your preaching has upon them. If we find it does them good, makes them honest and less disposed to cheat Indians, we will then consider again what you have said.[9]

These are the kinds of persons we are to "mark", those who act on what they say they believe. These people will,
- glorify God at every opportunity
- seek to align their lives by Scripture and not the other way around
- live the same at church and at home; in public and in private
- reveal their sincerity by the way they give of their time, their resources and their heart to those around them.
- show love toward others in the way they talk, the forgiveness they extend, and the consideration they show.

When you find a person that fulfills these characteristics . . . pay attention and learn all you can from them!

PRACTICALLY SPEAKING

As we look for good models for our lives we need to remember that the only model who is perfect is Jesus. Every model has weaknesses. Don't make your models into something they are not. Be aware of the weaknesses.

The best model is one who has been consistent over the "long haul". Anyone can look good for a little while. Some have said that the best models are those who have been dead for 100 years or so. That's good wisdom.

We must never put our models above the Bible. If your mentor does something contrary to scripture . . .think about getting another mentor!

Observe your models before you follow them. In the book of Hebrews we are given wise counsel, "*Remember your leaders, who spoke the word of God to you. Consider the outcome of their way of life and imitate their faith.*" (Hebrews 13:7) We must look at a person's life to see if they are worth following. This is the danger of making media leaders our models. We don't know how these people apply their Christianity. We don't know how they use their money. We don't know how they treat their families. We don't know how they react when they are frustrated. We don't know whether they do what they tell others to do.

The good models that Paul pointed to were people of character. A good model doesn't have to have rich talent, possess great knowledge, or have a faithful following. A good model is a person who has a heart for God. We must look past the surface things of life and look at a person's heart if we want to find models worth following.

Where do you find these good models? Let me give you some suggestions,

1. Study the life of Jesus and the apostles
2. Read biographies of those who have impacted the world for Christ (Billy Graham, Martin Luther, Charles Spurgeon, John Knox and many others)
3. Don't overlook the good models you may have in your

parents, grandparents, or siblings. Thank God if you have been blessed in such a way.

4. Look around at your fellow church members and note those who seem to live well for Christ. Get to know them and learn from their example.

Learn from your models and let them lead you to a deeper relationship with Christ. And as you live out your Christian lives do so carefully. Because you never know, someone may be watching you.

Study Questions

1. Who are some of the people who have been models to you? Why did you choose to make these people your model? Who do you know who would be a good person to make a model for your life? Why?
2. Why is it important for us to give attention to the models of our life? Do you agree that everyone has people they model their lives after?
3. Describe some bad models that you have known. What made them poor models? What "opened your eyes"?
4. What would it take for you to be a worthy model to others?
5. Who do you think are some of the best models from history? Why?

13

Living With Anticipation

Philippians 3:20-4:1

I've only traveled out of this country once in my life (If you don't count Canada). My college choir traveled in Germany, Denmark, Austria, and one glorious day in Switzerland. For one month between my freshman and sophomore years we enjoyed the adventure of Europe. We had a good time and experienced great hospitality but after one month every one of us was longing to return home. We were tired of having a new bed every night, of eating food that was unknown to us, and living in a world where we didn't understand what people were saying around us.

As we came approached Kennedy International Airport in New York we began listing all the things we had looked forward to,

- Soft toilet paper
- Fast food
- Sensible drivers
- American television
- English speaking merchants
- Our own beds

My parents spent a couple of years in Seoul, Korea due to my dad's business. In fact they were there during the time of the Seoul

Summer Olympics. During those two years my parents were very aware that they were foreigners. Customs were different, the food was different, and the language was different. Some people disliked my parents simply because they were Americans. After two years my parents were more than eager to return home.

Maybe you have served in the military and were stationed at a remote location. Whatever your military experience I bet it was good to get home. During your tour of duty I suspect you spent many nights thinking of and longing for what was at home.

Paul uses this kind of analogy to remind us that as believers, we are aliens and strangers in a foreign and hostile land. Our joy will never be fully realized until a future day. We won't know the full measure of joy until we get "home". Paul wrote to members of the church in Philippi,

> *Our citizenship is in heaven. And we eagerly await a Savior from there, the Lord Jesus Christ, who, by the power that enables him to bring everything under his control, will transform our lowly bodies so that they will be like his glorious body. Therefore, my brothers, you whom I love and long for, my joy and crown, that is how you should stand firm in the Lord, dear friends!* [Phil. 3:20-4:1]

WE ARE CITIZENS OF HEAVEN

Paul affirms that we are citizens of Heaven. Let me hasten to remind you that Paul is directing his comments to those he believes are sincere followers of Christ. He is not saying that *every* person is a citizen of Heaven. He does not even mean to imply that every person in the *church* is a citizen of Heaven. Paul believes he is talking to those who have received Christ as Savior and Lord. These people are citizens of Heaven by virtue of their relationship with Jesus. Only true believers can claim that they are really citizens of Heaven, on foreign duty.

Think about what this means. If we are truly citizens of Heaven, we don't belong here. As comfortable as we may be in this world, this is not our home. The values of this world are not our values. The treasures of this world are not our treasures.

If this world is not our home then it only figures that we will never find full satisfaction here. Sure, we can have a good time, we can enjoy our sojourn on the earth (and we should) but it's still not home.

For one summer I stayed in the home of a very loving, kind, and wonderfully generous family in Michigan. Al and Dorothy served as my hosts during a three-month ministry internship. These dear people worked hard to make me feel at home. They served food I enjoyed and provided comforts that I appreciated. But as warm and nice as they were, I just never was real comfortable in their house. It just wasn't home. I never felt comfortable raiding the refrigerator (mind you, I still did it . . . I just felt uneasy doing so). I never felt comfortable staying in their daughter's old bedroom (it was too "girly"). When I couldn't sleep I didn't really feel I could wander around the house. Their home was very comfortable, their spirits were wonderfully gracious, but it wasn't "home".

That's the way it is for the believer in the world. We will enjoy some of our times here on earth . . . but we will never really be home. There is a longing within us that will not be satisfied until we are with Jesus. God has planted that "ache" within us. He has placed a magnet in our soul drawing us toward heaven.

Paul wrote, "as it is written: *No eye has seen, no ear has heard, no mind has conceived what God has prepared for those who love him*" (1 Cor. 2:9). Do you know what this means? It means that no matter what you imagine Heaven to be, the reality is better than your imagination.

Do you imagine Heaven to be a place of endless happiness? Heaven is still better that that. Do you imagine Heaven to be a place where you live without fear, anxiety or pressure? Heaven is better still. Do you imagine Heaven as the best of family reunions? Keep trying . . . Heaven is better yet. Truthfully, we have no idea how wonderful Heaven is. What we do know is that Jesus will be there. And that reunion will be unimaginable in its greatness.

It would be appropriate as citizens of Heaven to
- spend much time thinking about Heaven.
- look forward to Heaven rather than fighting it.
- live our lives mindful that we represent another land and

strive to do so well.

- tell others about our home as often as we have opportunity.

WE ARE EAGERLY WAITING

The fact that we are citizens of Heaven leads us to look to Heaven. In fact, Paul says we are "eagerly waiting". He seems to point to two things we are eagerly waiting for.

For the Savior's return

When the disciples watched Jesus ascend to heaven after the resurrection and the forty days He spent with them, they stood with their mouths open looking at the sky. Two angels approached them and said, *"Men of Galilee, why do you stand here looking into the sky? This same Jesus, who has been taken from you into heaven, will come back in the same way you have seen him go into heaven."* (Acts 1:10-11) From those first moments after Jesus went to Heaven the followers of Christ have been anticipating His return.

There are many theories on how and when this coming will take place. Some say Jesus will come once in secret to get all the Christians and then will come again to judge the world after a period of intense persecution. This is the view made very popular by the Left Behind books.

There are other views that suggest that Christians will have to endure any persecution that comes but will be protected and defended by God's Spirit. Some say Christians will endure only part of the suffering. Others say there is no such thing as a secret rapture.

I find the whole debate rather confusing, and to be honest, I don't really care. What matters to me is the fact that Christ *will* return. That fact is one of the clearest doctrines of the New Testament. The church has always known that any moment Christ could come in glory and power.

The second coming is a central doctrine. Jesus talked of His return and the early church taught it with great expectation. We must remember that Bible prophecy wasn't given to us so that we could predict the future. It was given to us to stimulate our relationship with and confidence in God.

The second coming reminds us of several things,

- There will be a day of accounting . . .we must not conclude that anyone is "getting away with" anything
- There should be urgency in our witness and in our personal pursuit of holiness. We don't know how much time we have left.
- We must never look at world events and think that things are "out of control". The Lord's hands are still on the controls of time.

But we have to be honest. We confess and talk about our belief in the second coming but we *act* like we don't believe it. We live lives that seem unaffected by this great truth we proclaim. There is no change in our life. There is no urgency in our witness or our pursuit of holiness. Why is this?

First, it has been so long since Christ left the earth that we wonder if His promise to return is true. This is not a new problem. The first generation churches wondered also. Peter addressed the question then and his answer still is valid for us today,

> *But do not forget this one thing, dear friends: With the Lord a day is like a thousand years, and a thousand years are like a day. The Lord is not slow in keeping his promise, as some understand slowness. He is patient with you, not wanting anyone to perish, but everyone to come to repentance.* [2 Peter 3:8-9]

The Bible says that God is waiting until all who are going to believe come to faith. When that happens, the curtain will be drawn. We don't particularly like that answer because most of us aren't very patient. We want answers and we want them now! But, God's message is simple, "Be patient, I know what I am doing."

The second reason that we have a problem with the teaching of the second coming is sadly (but honestly) because we don't want it to be true. Most of us hope the Lord will come just as we are breathing our last breath . . . or at least wait until we are really old and can't get around any more. We are so attached to earth that we somehow imagine that His coming would "mess things up".

You don't believe me? Suppose Jesus were to return one hour from now. Take a minute to imagine that reality. What kinds of things come to mind? Maybe things like this,

- I won't get to see my baby born (imagine being pregnant for 8 ½ months when Jesus returns)
- I won't get to graduate from college
- I won't ever be married
- I won't be able to take the vacation I've already paid for
- I'll miss my child's birthday party
- I'll never see the Cubs win the World Series
- I won't know how the television drama cliffhanger ends

Yes, such thoughts are silly . . . we're going to Heaven!!! But we are so attached to the world that we want the Lord to delay His coming.

The Apostle Paul had a different attitude. He started every day wondering if "this would be the day" that the Lord was going to come in glory. He was eager because of what His coming would mean to Him.

For the transformation of the body

Paul was also looking forward to the transformation of the body. This is probably something that Paul thought about more than you or I do. Paul's body had a lot of wear on it. He had been beaten, imprisoned, stoned and left for dead. Paul said he had a "thorn in the flesh" which we are led to believe was some kind of physical ailment. In addition, Paul was getting older and with age comes new limits to your physical ability.

Heaven is where the effects of aging are turned around. The aching joints are spry again; the lack of balance is replaced with sure-footedness; fuzzy memories give way to clear recollections; an inability to speak will be replaced with fluent praise. In that day the extra weight we couldn't shake will be gone; the cataracts will give way to clarity, and the general weakness of the years will be replaced with vitality.

The Bible likens our resurrected body to the transformation that takes place when a seed is planted in the ground, or when a caterpillar comes out of the cocoon as a butterfly. The human metamorphosis that will take place is something that we can't presently fathom.

This is why we long for His coming. When Christ comes our inheritance will be revealed. The transformation will take place. The glory will be revealed.

WE MUST STAND FIRM

Therefore, my brothers, you whom I love and long for, my joy and crown, that is how you should stand firm in the Lord, dear friends! [4:1]

The Apostle Paul gives us a "therefore". It's his conclusion to all that is said. Because Christ is coming again, and because we are looking forward to a day when He will transform our earthly bodies, we should be standing firm. These great truths should give us stability in life and they should be the anchors that hold us steady in the difficult storms of life.

For the anchors to hold, we must remember our Lord's promise to return and live our lives in light of His return. We must take it seriously.

PRACTICALLY SPEAKING

Paul's words are not just theological trivia. The hope that Paul talks about is practical. So, as we conclude let me ask you some pointed questions,

1. How would your life be different if you believed Jesus was coming today?
2. Are you living as a citizen of Heaven or are you denying your citizenship by the way you live?
3. Are you putting more emphasis on your earthly body than you should? Do you remember that our bodies are to be tools to honor the Lord and not an end in itself? Are you spending more time caring for your temporal body than you are for your eternal soul?
4. Do you believe in Heaven? Are you investing in Heaven or are you spending everything you have on the things of this life.

Some people say that Christians can be so heavenly minded that they are no earthly good. But that isn't true. It is true that some people can be so *self-righteous* that they are no earthly good. They feel such a sense of superiority over others that they can't be *bothered* with the practical aspects of ministry. There are people who spend so much time in speculation and arguing over theological minutiae that they never seem to get around to living the Christian life.

But a person who is truly heavenly minded is a person who is working hard to make a difference in the world. This person is not only the most joyful person; they are also working hardest to minister to the people around them. And do you know why this is the case? It's because the person who is truly heavenly minded, is most aware of what is at stake.

So enjoy your time in this foreign land but don't forget that you aren't home yet.

Discussion Questions

1. Have you ever traveled to a foreign land? Where did you go? How long were you there? What were your feelings as you returned home?
2. Why do you think Christians spend so little time actually thinking about Heaven or the implications of the Second Coming of Jesus? Do you think we really *don't* want Jesus to return today?
3. What do you imagine Heaven to be like? What do you look forward to most about heaven?
4. How can we help each other to be more "heavenly minded"?
5. What kinds of things do you think a truly "heavenly minded person" would do?

14

Getting Along with Others in the Church

Philippians 4:2,3

If you have ever been part of a conflict in a church family you know how painful it can be. Churches split, friends divide, and competing sides charge the other with being "unchristian". The self-righteousness of the conflict makes it even more difficult to resolve. Church conflicts bring about deep scars in the body of Christ. In every church congregation today there are people who have been hindered in their spiritual growth because of a church conflict at one time in their life.

The effects of church conflict are not only internal. The conflict inevitably makes its way into the public spotlight. Non-Christian people see the way the Christians bicker and conclude that all the talk about love is merely a veneer. Our reputation is stained in the community and the Lord is saddened.

In His High Priestly Prayer Jesus prayed for his followers to be one like He and the Father were. He told His disciples to "love one another". In the Sermon on the Mount Jesus told his listeners that if they were offering their gift at the altar and remembered that someone had something against them, they were to get up and leave the gift at the altar and first go and be reconciled to their brother. Jesus understood that it is difficult to worship when you are at odds with someone else. God wants us to get along.

In Philippians 4, the apostle Paul makes a personal plea for reconciliation in the church.

> *I plead with Euodia and I plead with Syntyche to agree with each other in the Lord. Yes, and I ask you, loyal yokefellow, help these women who have contended at my side in the cause of the gospel, along with Clement and the rest of my fellow workers, whose names are in the book of life.*

It appears that there was a problem with two women in the church, Euodia and Syntyche. Since these women are not mentioned elsewhere in the Bible, it is impossible to know the nature of the problem. We may not know what the problem is, but we can guess that as so often happens, the people in the church were being asked to choose sides in the dispute. We can only imagine the situation in the church,

- groups met in corners and talked about how carnal the other side was becoming
- every conversation turned to the conflict
- instead of a feeling of peace in their worship there was a tension that was threatening to make the time of worship a meaningless activity because the conflict occupied the attention of everyone.
- any little disagreement was a potential match that could result in an explosion disproportionate to the issue. Pressure was building to dangerous levels.

I think it was because of these practical realities that the Apostle Paul pleads for these women to agree with one another. He asks the loyal yokefellow to lend a hand in mediating this problem. We don't know who this "loyal yokefellow" is, but it is interesting that Paul implies that sometimes you need a mediator in resolving a conflict.

As we look through the Bible at this issue of conflict there are six truths that will help us to live at peace with each other.

Conflict Happens

It may seem like I am stating the obvious, but sometimes the obvious needs to be stated. Euodia and Syntyche were loyal followers of Christ. Paul says they were among those who contended at his side. These women were not non-Christian people who were in the church. They were genuine followers.

Christians are new creatures in Christ but they still have some of the old ways about them: personalities still clash; we still get our feelings hurt; we have times when we may feel a little overwhelmed (making us more irritable); people still disappoint us; and people have different approaches to solving problems. Some are aggressive and confrontational, some let conflict eat away at them until they explode. Christians are still people! And whenever you have two people together there is a potential for conflict.

There are times in the Christian community when others ARE wrong and in love we have to address the wrong and this often leads to hard feelings. I don't think it is sinful that we sometimes rub each other the wrong way . . . that is being human. What is sinful is the way we often handle those times.

Let me give you a rather embarrassing example from my own life. I was a hot-shot seminary student working at a suburban church outside Chicago. I was making a very modest sum for working with the youth and helping in the educational areas. I also taught an adult Sunday School class.

This particular church had one worship service and Sunday School met during the worship time. As a result of this set-up the children were not in worship and adults had little opportunity for the interaction and fellowship of a Bible Class. I met with a class after worship when everyone else had gone home.

The people in my class (certainly at my prodding) began to feel that the Sunday School hour should be separate from the worship hour. After much discussion my class brought the matter before the board and then before the congregation. In our zeal to do what we felt was best for the church, we pushed the issue. And we pushed hard. Whenever someone feels they are being backed into a corner, they will resist. And that's what happened.

Eventually, the issue came to a congregational vote. I was not even a member of the church at this time and I was asked to leave the meeting. The church voted against changing the time for Sunday School. I suspect many voted "no" not because they really cared about Sunday School but because they didn't like being pushed.

As a result of this "heated" meeting some of the young families left the church. The church was wounded and I was responsible. My ego caused me to encourage a confrontation and this led to division rather than growth. I chose to stir up conflict rather than take the time to do the hard work of working through the issue one person at a time. (After I left to be a Pastor, the church did move Sunday School to a time separate from the worship service. This was small consolation to me.)

In my situation, Christian people were trying to do what was right but did it in the wrong way. Conflict often can arise even out of good intentions.

Conflict is Costly

It is interesting that Paul does not indicate who is right and who is wrong in the conflict with Euodia and Syntche. Paul simply pleads for them to "agree with each other in the Lord." The implication is quite obvious: if they were "in the Lord" they would work at finding agreement; they would work through their problems. In fact, it seems that Paul is saying that "for the sake of the Lord" they should agree. When Christians fight with each other several things happen
- the Lord's reputation is harmed
- the Church's ministry is hampered
- the body of Christ is handicapped
- personal peace is affected
- and we move away from God's heart

Paul scolded the Corinthians,

If any of you has a dispute with another, dare he take

it before the ungodly for judgment instead of before the saints? Do you not know that the saints will judge the world? And if you are to judge the world, are you not competent to judge trivial cases? Do you not know that we will judge angels? How much more the things of this life! Therefore, if you have disputes about such matters, appoint as judges even men of little account in the church! I say this to shame you. Is it possible that there is nobody among you wise enough to judge a dispute between believers? But instead, one brother goes to law against another— and this in front of unbelievers! The very fact that you have lawsuits among you means you have been completely defeated already. Why not rather be wronged? Why not rather be cheated? Instead, you yourselves cheat and do wrong, and you do this to your brothers. [1 Corinthians. 6:1-8]

Paul recognized that we will have disputes. However, he argued that Christians should be able to resolve their conflicts without having to parade their dirty laundry before the rest of the world. If there is a problem, we should seek to work things out between us. If that doesn't work, we should try to find an arbitrator in the church who can help us resolve things in a Christian manner.

In his words to the Corinthians, Paul makes the bold statement that we should rather be wronged than bring a stain to the church and our Lord by making our conflict public. In our litigious society such an attitude seems un-American! Paul sees unity as such an important issue that we should go to any extreme to maintain it.

We Must Take Responsibility for Our Own Behavior

The one thing you can be sure of in any conflict situation is this: it was always the other person's fault! We are very good at spotting the faults of others but very poor at accepting responsibility for our own failures. In the Sermon on the Mount Jesus warned people not to judge others until they had taken the log out of their own eye. In times of conflict we should always begin by asking, "What responsibility do I have for this conflict."

Paul urges both of these women to work at reconciliation. Both were at fault. It doesn't matter what kind of conflict is taking place, we certainly have some culpability in the situation. There are a number of good questions to ask yourself when you are in a conflict situation

1. Have I fueled this conflict by my own pride, stubbornness or defensiveness?
2. Have I contributed to this conflict by hurtful words, aggressive tactics, or by twisting what really happened?
3. Have I refused to give someone the benefit of the doubt and instead concluded that I know what the motives of another really are?
4. Have I hindered reconciliation by my bitterness, evil thoughts, or stubbornness?
5. Am I acting like I have no responsibility for the problems that exist?
6. Am I guilty of resisting God by refusing to extend forgiveness and seek reconciliation?
7. Am I guilty of perpetuating this conflict by my laziness?
8. Am I waiting for the other person to make the first move and thus violating Paul's command to do everything that we can do to be reconciled?

It is amazing how fast reconciliation can come to a situation when people are honestly willing to admit and address their responsibility for a conflict situation. As we look at our own hearts and attitudes we are taking a step toward reconciliation. We are beginning to remove the barrier that exists between us and another person.

We Should Commit the Matter to Prayer

One of the best ways of getting to the heart of our responsibility and obligation is to turn to prayer. An amazing thing happens when we begin to pray. We come before the Lord and present our argument that justifies why we are angry. We say, "O Lord, Woe is me . . . I have been treated so shamefully . . ." I have found that the

Lord listens for a while and then begins to turn the searchlight on my own attitudes and actions. He shows me where I have been petty, insensitive and cold. In short, He begins to show me the log in my own eye. In these times the Lord has shown me (much to my chagrin) that,

- I was being unrealistic in my expectations
- I was expecting people to meet expectations I never told them about
- I was expecting people to care about the same things I cared about
- I was defending my "glory" and not His
- I was being petty

These are not pleasant revelations, but they are necessary. When you take a conflict situation to the Lord in honest and open prayer, He will start by addressing *your* responsibility in the conflict. After you have seen your responsibility, the Lord will begin to urge you to do what is right. God may urge us to "let it go", to forgive, to go and talk to the person about the problem, and He may even push us to apologize for our own wrong-doing.

Much of the time when we pray about a conflict situation we aren't really asking for God's help to resolve the conflict, we are lobbying God to be on our side! We want God to change the other person.

I have found that I can resist this searchlight of the Lord for a long time but not forever. I can feel pretty self-righteous. But while I do so I am resisting the whispers of His Spirit about my own responsibility for the conflict. During this time I lose that peace that surpasses comprehension, my relationship with the Lord is strained, and I have trouble sleeping. I try to justify my actions but the more I resist, the more pressure He puts on me. The Lord won't let us get away with ignoring the truth.

In many of Jesus' parables he reminds us that we are sinful people ourselves, and if it wasn't for God's forgiveness we would not be able to stand. In fact, God will remind us that our sin before God is so much greater than the sin that others have committed against us. At times I sense the Lord asking, "O.K. do you want to treat others the way I have treated you? Or, would you rather I treat you the way you treat others?" Once God gets us to this point, we are usually ready to listen.

Extend Grace Where Possible
Solomon wrote,

> A man's wisdom gives him patience; it is to his glory to overlook an offense. [Pr. 19:11]
> A fool shows his annoyance at once, but a prudent man overlooks an insult. [Pr. 12:16]
> Starting a quarrel is like breaching a dam; so drop the matter before a dispute breaks out. [Pr. 17:14]

Paul told the Colossians,

> *Therefore, as God's chosen people, holy and dearly loved, clothe yourselves with compassion, kindness, humility, gentleness and patience. Bear with each other and forgive whatever grievances you may have against one another. Forgive as the Lord forgave you.* [Col. 3:12-13]

There are many molehills that we make into mountains. A little issue can easily become a big deal. If we want to be people who reflect God's love in our relationships with each other, then we must be willing to overlook offenses. Some things that offend us should just be overlooked.

We all have bad days and bad moments. We are all irritable at times and in those times we are often offensive to others. We feel "stressed out" so we over-react to every little thing. It's a fact of life. We must be willing to accept the humanity of the other person just like we accept our own humanity. We must be willing to extend the same grace to others that we hope they will extend to us.

Instead of continuing a feud, say "Hi" or extend your hand. Instead of avoiding someone go right up to them and ask them "how are you doing?" Do something to break the ice. Maybe you can send a "Thinking about You" card or write a note for a special day. If you have made a molehill into a mountain do something to put things back into perspective.

Lower the "Temperature"

In Proverbs we are told, "a soft answer turns away wrath". Calmness and gentleness lead to reconciliation. Aggressiveness and harshness lead to more deeply entrenched battles. This counsel is just the opposite of the counsel we get from the world. The common advice it to "stand up for our rights." We are taught to be more assertive, more aggressive, and more antagonistic. These are unbiblical approaches and yet, we seem to feel being aggressive and "no-nonsense" is a badge of honor and something to be proud of.

Aggressiveness results in making the other person defensive rather than open; it puts us in attack mode rather than reconciling mode; it makes us resistant to God's instruction; and words are spoken that are designed to wound rather than heal

If you see that you are becoming aggressive, you know that you need to get alone with the Lord and work things out. When there is a need to confront a problem it is always good to do several things,

- Affirm the positive
- Confess your own responsibility honestly and specifically
- Explain rather than attack
- Wait for your anger to cool
- Refrain from words like "always" and "never"
- Keep focused on the main issue
- Work towards reconciliation, not blame
- Speak softly

We must be "under control" ourselves before there can be any hope of reconciliation. We can determine the temperature of the conflict. If one person is willing to discuss but refuses to argue, there is hope for understanding.

One time I found myself in the middle of a big argument in our community. I was appointed to a committee just at the time they were beginning a very controversial discussion. I tried to keep an open mind but ended up "in the sights" of one of the antagonists.

One morning this antagonist called me at my office and immediately began attacking. I told this man that I was happy to discuss this with him but I wasn't going to fight with him. He continued to attack. I hung up the phone.

I knew what was going to happen. In five minutes the man was at my office door. He said, "Something must have happened . . . we were cut off." I said, "We weren't cut off, I hung up on you!" He was surprised by my calmness and straightforwardness.

He asked why I would hang up on him. I told him that I had meant what I said. I would be happy to discuss matters with him, but I wasn't going to fight. I told him that if he would like to talk we could talk but if he wanted to fight, I had better things to do.

During the next hour we discussed the issue. Both of us were able to express our concerns and I think we came to realize that we both were seeking the best for our community. We may not have completely agreed on everything but we were able to respect each other's position.

Practically Speaking

I hope I have given you some practical things to think about and put into practice in conflict situations. One of the best ways to show that our Christianity is genuine is in the way we handle conflict. God can change us . . . if we let Him. We can learn to be peacemakers rather than troublemakers. We can become soft rather than abrasive. We not only CAN . . . we MUST. The stakes are high. The world is watching.

I'm not suggesting that we will resolve every conflict. Paul told us that "as far is it depends on you, be at peace with all men." Sometimes the other person doesn't want to listen. Sometimes they don't want reconciliation. Sometimes the issues are too big to simply shrug them off. Sometimes our disagreements are over essential points of doctrine. In these times we can only walk away and hope for an opportunity to be reconciled some time in the future. But we must not do this too quickly! We must work and work hard at being reconciled before concluding that there is nothing more we can do.

So, examine the situations that keep you churning. Take another look at the things you are bitter about. Rather than stoking the fires of resentment, look at *your* responsibility. Are you at fault in some way? Are you guilty of making a mountain out of a molehill? Is there something you can and should do to mend this relationship?

It is easier to walk away. It is easier to blame others for every-thing. But it is not the Savior's way. He wants us to be one. He wants us to work together and to help each other. I guess what I'm saying is this: You may not care about you relationship with your antagonist. But God does.

Discussion Questions

1. What is the issue in the worst conflict situation you have ever witnessed? How was the conflict handled? What were the long term results?
2. Do you think conflict is inevitable? Why?
3. Why do we have such a hard time seeing our own responsi-bility for the times of conflict?
4. What ideas were new in this chapter? What ideas were the most helpful? Which do you think would be the most diffi-cult to practice?
5. What lessons have you learned through some of the conflict situations of your life? Positive lessons? Negative lessons?

15

Getting Rid of the Sharp Edges

Philippians 4:5

After every tragic shooting that has taken place in a high school in America we have heard the same testimony again and again. The assailant(s) were children who had been bullied and ridiculed by the others in their school and community. They had been tormented to the point that they had enough and decided to strike back.

Most of us have been on the receiving end of unkind comments at one time or another. We looked different; we weren't as talented, attractive, and intelligent as those around us, and we were ridiculed. Some have been ridiculed for their weight, their appearance, their intelligence, their awkwardness, and even (maybe even especially) their burdens. Some have had physical problems, others came from difficult home situations but all were picked on nonetheless. If you have ever felt that pain, if you ever knew what it was like to not want to go to school (or work) because of the rejection and hatred you would experience, then you understand how devastating such things are. You may even understand the pain that might cause someone to snap.

Maybe you have been the abuser. I look back on my days in 8th grade and am ashamed. We had someone's precious daughter in our class. She had a deformity that left one leg shorter than the other. She also had a weight problem and didn't talk as well as others. Rather than befriend her, much of the class tormented her. Rather than find out her story, we made her an object of abuse. I don't know that I ever said anything directly to her, but I'm sure I laughed at the jokes (which weren't funny) and I certainly did nothing to make her feel that she had a friend. And to this day, I can remember what we called her, but I can't remember her name. I wish I could beg her forgiveness for the hurt.

The more in tune we become with the realities of the world, the more we will marvel at the wisdom of God's Word. In the midst of Paul's discussion on joy he gives us Philippians 4:5. It is almost as if Paul realized that one of the greatest hindrances to joy is the scars that have come from the bullies of life. So he writes, "Let your gentleness be evident to all. The Lord is near."

In a mean, abusive, insensitive culture, we are to be gentle. This reminds us that our Christianity is not primarily about theology exams or Bible knowledge . . . it is about the change that comes about when God's Spirit takes up residence in our lives. That change is practical. It is a change that should affect every area of our life, and especially our dealings with others.

Verse five is a difficult verse to translate because the word translated "gentleness" has a number of different shades of meaning.

> Let everyone see that you are considerate in all you (NLT)
> Let your moderation be known unto all men. (KJV)
> Let your forbearance be known unto all men. (NASB)
> Make it as clear as you can to all you meet that you're on their side, working with them and not against them. (The Message)

From these various meanings I think we can draw some lessons on how to bring joy by our words and actions.

WE SHOULD RESPECT THOSE AROUND US

Novelist Frank Peretti wrote a deeply personal book called THE WOUNDED SPIRIT. Peretti tells the story of his life and the pain he endured because of his physical deformities. He draws some powerful lessons from his own experiences. You can't read this book and be the same ever again. Peretti writes,

> . . .bullying and abuse betray a lack or loss of respect for other human beings, there is a deeper issue: the devaluing of human life; and that in turn indicates a lack or loss of respect for the Giver of human life and dignity, God Himself. The message a bully sends is a mockery of God's handiwork, a lie that slanders God's nature and negates His love for us.[10]

We show a lack of respect when we treat other people like objects rather than as human beings. And when we do this we not only show a lack of respect toward others, we show that we do not respect God who created the others and declared them valuable. People who do not respect others think only of themselves.

Showing consideration and respect for others begins in very little things,

- like picking up after yourself so someone else doesn't have to
- letting another go in front of you in a line
- refusing to ridicule another
- being friendly to someone who is tired or alone
- respecting the time of another by being on time for appointments
- only taking up one parking spot
- replacing the roll when it is empty
- listening when another person is talking.

Learning to be considerate in the little things will maybe help us in the big things. The little things are just little things but they are important. If we are not faithful in the little things, Jesus said, we would not be faithful in bigger things.

We should be considerate for several reasons,

- it's the way of Christ

- we know the pain of being on the other side of the ridicule
- it is the human thing to do
- it is the way you would want others to treat you
- it's right

Why are we the way we are? Why is it so easy to start ridiculing another? Why do we laugh at another's expense? Why do we join in the taunting when everyone is being unkind to someone whether he or she is present or not? Where is that evidence of the Spirit of God in us at these times? I wonder if these are the times when God's Spirit grieves.

Peretti suggests that part of the problem is our current worldview. If there is no God then there is no absolute truth, if there is no absolute truth, then there is no standard of right and wrong. If there is no standard of right and wrong, decency gives way to barbarity. Christians must take the lead in bringing values back into our society.

True Christian love is revealed in the every day events of life. Christian love is not about lyrics in a song . . . it is about the way we treat others. James wrote, *"Whoever considers himself to be religious but does not keep a tight rein on his tongue, deceives himself and his religion is empty."* (James 1:26)

WE SHOULD BE PATIENT WITH DIFFICULT PEOPLE AND CIRCUMSTANCES

The word forbearance means to bear up under a burden. It is where the idea of patience comes from. We are to be patient with our circumstances and with people. This is not the only place where Paul makes this assertion,

> *Be joyful in hope, patient in affliction, faithful in prayer.* [Romans 12:12-13]
> *love is patient, and love is kind* [1 Corinthians 13:4]
> *Be completely humble and gentle; be patient, bearing with one another in love.* [Ephesians 4:2]

If you spend any time with people, you know that patience is not something that is in large supply. Someone has suggested that our society has developed a new unit of time called the honko-second.

This is the short period of time between when the light changes to green and the person behind you honks their horn. Everyone seems to be in a hurry. Let's take a little quiz and see how you are doing in the area of patience?

1. Do you ever feel annoyed that the person in front of you is *only* driving the speed limit?
2. Do you ever become perturbed when the person in front of you in the check out line is writing a check and doesn't start writing until everything is totaled?
3. Do get angry if someone isn't ready to listen the instant you are ready to talk?
4. Do you get frustrated if some project doesn't go well right away?
5. Do you find yourself yelling at traffic lights?
6. Do you ever pace while waiting for the coffee pot to finish or the toast to pop?
7. Are you irritated when you have to wait in a waiting room?
8. Does it annoy you when you are walking down an aisle in a store and an older person (or a mother with her children) keeps you from walking as fast as you would like to walk?

My family smiles at this little quiz because they know that I flunk every one of these things. I'll admit that I am still in the patience classroom.

I've come to believe if we want to develop more patience we must think more theologically about life. Before you dismiss that thought, let me explain. We must remind ourselves that circumstances come our way for a purpose. We need to believe that God really is in control. We need to believe the words of Romans 8:28, "In all things God is working for the good of those who love him and are called according to His purpose."

If we take these things seriously then we will see every frustrating occurrence as an opportunity for growth. When we are frustrated we will step back and ask, "How can I honor the Lord in this situation?"

When I am behind a slow driver or a person taking what seems to be a long time at a check-out lane, I try to remind myself that this is an opportunity for me to learn to trust. It is a chance given to me by God to develop that patience I always seem to be lacking. I ask myself, "What's the hurry?" I like to call these frustrating times my spiritual homework. If we learn to think theologically (really believe that God is involved in our lives) we will be more patient with others.

Secondly, if we are going to be patient with others we must learn to give people room to grow.

> Impatient people have an inflated view of them- selves, having lost the capacity to see themselves as sinners in the process of becoming saints. They also have a bad memory. They have forgotten about all the foolish decisions they made, the stupid things they said to others, the petty concerns that occupied their minds. Every so often we need to be reminded of what we once were and how undesirable it was. Many people have been forbearing toward us—our parents, children, teachers, friends, associates. Is it any surprise that God commands us to do the same for others? A sober view of ourselves will make us much quicker to put up with the immaturity of others.[11]

We want others to be patient with us as we mature and grow . . . so we should extend the same courtesy to others. We must constantly remind ourselves of several important factors.

Sometimes there are factors we don't know about. We may not realize that the person who is so obnoxious is just looking for some- one to accept them. The person who is driving well under the speed limit may just be learning to drive, or maybe they recently had an accident, or maybe they aren't seeing very well. Or maybe they actually think that as a Christian a speed law should be obeyed.

We also need to remember that *growth takes time*. We may be frustrated with how clumsy someone is in a certain area (in which we are proficient) and forget how long it took us to become proficient. (We see this especially as parents teach their children how to drive).

Impatience never makes things better. If you are running late for something and begin to get impatient with the people around you, does it help? No, it just complicates the situation more and makes the circumstance that much more miserable.

People who learn to be patient with others will find that they have an easier time being patient with themselves. Impatient people make unrealistic demands not only on others but also on themselves.

WE ARE TO RELATE TO OTHERS WITH KINDNESS AND SOFTNESS

We must be kind and soft in our dealings with others. We are to remember that we represent Jesus. Matthew applied these words of Isaiah to Jesus, *"He will not quarrel or cry out; no one will hear his voice in the streets. A bruised reed he will not break, and a smoldering wick he will not snuff out, till he leads justice to victory. In his name the nations will put their hope."* (Matthew 12:19-21) The New Living Translation says, *" He will not crush those who are weak, or quench the smallest hope."* Jesus was sensitive to the hurting and tender with them.

On a practical note, kindness opens people up while harshness shuts them up. I have found when I attack someone they either back away or fight back. Neither response is productive. The more sarcastic I become (and I can be pretty sarcastic) the more the target of my sarcasm is going to resist. If you are sarcastic with a waitress there is a good chance your service will be worse rather than better. If you are aggressive with a sales person they will tell you to take your business elsewhere.

On the flip side of this scenario, I have found softness and kindness can help diffuse even the most volatile situations. A calm tone, a soft word, and a warm smile can do wonders to lower the hostilities around us. Solomon is right (of course) *"a soft answer does turn away wrath"*. A kind word does bring down barriers.

I have discovered from my dealings with police officers, hospital staff and other business people, that people are much more helpful and forthcoming when I am soft. If I try to "flex my muscles" other people will try to show they are stronger than I am. They will refuse to cooperate. However, if I am soft, gentle, and understanding, people have been more than willing to give me whatever information or help I need.

Our goal is to be soft rather than harsh. The soft person is secure in their relationship with Christ and doesn't have to view every encounter as a contest. The soft person is aware of grace and the undeserved kindness they have received from the Lord. Remember Paul's sober warning, "*You, therefore have no excuse, you who pass judgment on another. For at whatever point you judge the other, you are condemning yourself. For you who pass judgment do the same things.*" (Romans 2:1) When we judge a person by their weakness we are inviting God to judge us by our weaknesses!

I am concerned about the rising aggressiveness I see in the Christian community. The church seems to be trying to become a political powerbroker. More and more it seems we are trying to "flex our muscle" to get our way. Please understand, I think we must stand up for what we believe in. I think we should use resources at our disposal. But we must stand up for truth in a way that conveys the love of Christ! We cannot and will not be able to legislate moral behavior. We must first model that behavior. Unfortunately many in the world have concluded that some of the nastiest people in the world are Christians.

WE SHOULD LEAD BALANCED LIVES

Gentleness also includes the idea of moderation. Moderation has to do with justice. The person who is showing moderation is one who does not always insist on justice but is willing to extend mercy and grace. It would have been justice for Jesus to condemn the woman caught in adultery. But instead He acted in mercy and told her to "go and sin no more." He didn't compromise with sin, but He also didn't apply the harshest penalty.

Moderation involves maintaining balance in our lives. We are to be champions of truth, yet extenders of mercy. We are to uphold God's standards while reaching out to those who have turned their backs on God's values. In other words, we must live in the harsh world by the values of Heaven. That takes balance.

The story is told that Ghandi one day was getting on board a train. As he got on the train (which was already beginning to move) one of his shoes slipped off and landed on the track. He couldn't retrieve the shoe so, to the amazement of his friends, he took off the other one and threw it back on the track also. When those around him asked why he did that, he replied, "Now the poor man who finds the shoe will have a pair he can use." Here was a man who wasn't even a Christian who had balance in his life.

PRACTICALLY SPEAKING

There are two additional things we need to learn from Paul's words, "*Let your gentleness be evident to all. The Lord is near.*" First, consider the **parameters of the instruction.** We are told that we are to act this way to ALL people. It's easy to be nice, kind, patient, gentle and controlled with some people. It's not so easy with others. But Paul does not leave us a loophole. We are to be this way to everyone. If Paul were here, he might add we are to be gentle "especially" with the difficult people. We are to be this way with the false teacher, the person of another faith, the person who has an abrasive personality. We aren't to compromise truth (we can be kind without giving away truth) but we are to be kind. This is a marvelous way to disarm our enemies.

Second, notice the **motivation for the instructions**. We do these things because we realize that the Lord is near. This can mean two things. First, it may mean that we are to act with gentleness because the time is short. Paul may be saying that the second coming of the Lord is near. If this is the case, we don't have time to waste on the petty things of life. There is too much at stake. We are better off to absorb the stinging arrows of another rather than risk pushing them away with our demeanor.

But the text also could mean that we should act this way because the Lord is ALWAYS near. Paul may simply be reminding us that the Lord is present with us in every circumstance and every relationship. We are to be kind and compassionate and patient because we are in the Lord's company. Let's face it, there are times during our life that we do things we would never do in church. Why? We have this sense that God is watching us in church. But Paul wants us to remember that God is watching us everywhere we go!

We live in a world that seems to be spinning out of control. Bullying and violence are on the rise. In response, people raise their hands in despair. They blame guns, they blame television, they blame the news media and they blame the government. Why is it that no one seems to see the problem clearly? Why do some people feel they have the right to treat others poorly simply because they are bigger, or stronger, or older, or have more power?

We have lost our anchor of truth. We have tossed away the idea that we are created in the image of God. We have forgotten that God has called us to respect, honor, and love one another. We have forgotten that Jesus tells us that we show our love for Him by the way we relate to the weakest in our society.

You and I need to be leaders in bringing about the change that needs to take place. Before the *world* will remember the value of an individual, the *church* must do so. Before the church can do so, individual Christians must take God's commands seriously. We must be the ones who defend the weak rather than exploit them. We must be the ones who show love rather than force. We must be the ones who are kind rather than aggressive. We must be the ones who refuse to be party with those who ridicule others. We must adopt the tactics of Jesus rather than the tactics of the world. And when we do this, we must pray that the world sees what we are doing. . . .and then follows our example.

Discussion Questions

1. What hurtful things can you remember doing in your life? If you are able to talk about it, what scars do you carry with your from the times when you were the one hurt?
2. In what way does our harshness with others reveal a lack of respect for God?
3. Do you think there is ever a time when Christians can be aggressive and loving? Are there times when an aggressive attitude will be more productive than gentleness?
4. What kinds of people are most difficult to relate to with gentleness? (This answer will be different for different people)
5. In what circumstances do you find yourself most impatient?
6. Which of the suggestions in this chapter do you need to work on first?

16

The Antidote to Anxiety

Philippians 4:6,7

Have you ever had a time in your life when things were so over-whelming that you could not sleep? Have there been times when you were so preoccupied with a problem that you didn't seem to be able to function? Have there been issues of your life that seem to dominate every waking thought? If so, you have known anxiety. When anxiety takes residence in our lives, joy moves out.

Chuck Swindoll calls worry the "universal addiction". Paul understood the natural tendency to become anxious. He realized that anxiety is one of the greatest thieves of joy. Because of this Paul wrote,

> *Do not be anxious about anything, but in everything,*
> *by prayer and petition, with thanksgiving, present*
> *your requests to God. And the peace of God, which*
> *transcends all understanding, will guard your hearts*
> *and your minds in Christ Jesus.* (Philippians 4:6,7)

THE PROHIBITION

Don't you hate when people tell you not to worry? It is so easy for someone to say and a lot harder to do. Sometimes we feel that

179

the person who is telling you not to worry is the one who doesn't fully comprehend the problem, because if they did, they would be worried too!

In Matthew 6 Jesus condemned worry. He says worry is foolish and shows a lack of confidence in the person, character, and ability of God. Listen to the words of Jesus

> *"Therefore I tell you, do not worry about your life, what you will eat or drink; or about your body, what you will wear. Is not life more important than food, and the body more important than clothes? Look at the birds of the air; they do not sow or reap or store away in barns, and yet your heavenly Father feeds them. Are you not much more valuable than they? Who of you by worrying can add a single hour to his life?*
>
> *"And why do you worry about clothes? See how the lilies of the field grow. They do not labor or spin. Yet I tell you that not even Solomon in all his splendor was dressed like one of these. If that is how God clothes the grass of the field, which is here today and tomorrow is thrown into the fire, will he not much more clothe you, O you of little faith? So do not worry, saying, 'What shall we eat?' or 'What shall we drink?' or 'What shall we wear?' For the pagans run after all these things, and your heavenly Father knows that you need them. But seek first his kingdom and his righteousness, and all these things will be given to you as well.* (Mt. 6:25-33)

So why is worry wrong? Jesus gives us several reasons. **First, It puts the focus on the wrong issues**. Jesus said, "Is not life more important than food?" When we worry, our perspective becomes skewed. We begin to focus on things that are secondary and in the process lose sight of what is really important. Let me give you some examples,

- You are so worried about a graduation party that you miss the joy that comes from the accomplishment of graduating.

- You worry so much about the winter weather that you don't enjoy the Christmas holiday with family (I'm guilty of this one)
- You worry so much about looking good at a gathering that you become so absorbed with yourself that you can't enjoy the people around you.
- You are so worried about not having enough money that you don't enjoy the journey of life.
- You are so worried about how you are doing (in an interview, speech, etc.) that you come across tense and forced.

Worry distorts our thinking. When we worry, we tend to look at situations through a magnifying glass making things bigger than they really are. Molehills become mountains.

Second, **worry causes us to lose sight of whom we belong to**. Jesus argues that God is more than capable of taking care of us. He cares for the birds, the flowers, and the animals. When we worry, we show that we think that we are less important to God than these things. We aren't. God will take care of us. Jesus tells us that God knows what we need. And because God knows what we need He will take care of His children. In another parable about prayer Jesus says,

> *"Which of you, if his son asks for bread, will give him a stone? Or if he asks for a fish, will give him a snake? If you, then, though you are evil, know how to give good gifts to your children, how much more will your Father in heaven give good gifts to those who ask him!* [Matthew 7:7-9]

If God knows what we need (and He does), it is inconceivable to think that God will not meet those needs if we trust Him rather than our own devices.

Do you know what the greatest help has been for me when it comes to anxiety? It is this truth: "Worry is sin". When we are anxious it reveals that we really don't trust God. It shows that either we believe God is not capable, or that God does not care. Neither is true. So when I realize that I am beginning to be filled with anxiety, I ask myself an important question, "Do I trust God, or don't I?"

Third, **worry is a fruitless activity**. Jesus said, "Who by worry can add a single hour to his life." Worry is wasted energy. There is nothing productive about worry. It leads nowhere. Worry hinders us rather than helps us. Worry paralyzes rather than energizes us.

Worry robs us of energy and often has very negative effects: our health suffers (ulcers, blood pressure, heart problems, colon distress, headaches); we don't get enough rest because we don't sleep well; we become irritable to be around and begin to see only the clouds on a sunny day. Worry keeps us from being able to address the issues we can and should be doing something about.

THE PRESCRIPTION

Most of us know that worry is wrong. The problem we face is that we don't know how to combat this very human tendency. Paul tells us to eliminate worry by prayer. We are to pray about everything (no exceptions). In other words, there is no problem, no circumstance, and no situation that cannot be brought before the Father. We are to hide nothing from Him.

Do you see the wisdom? Rather than talk to ourselves and get all worked up (Worry is like wearing a groove in the snow with your tires. The more you spin your tires the deeper (and slicker) the rut becomes), we are to talk to God. Do you get it? When you start to fret, when you start to get yourself churning over something, it is time to talk to the Lord. Prayer is a worshipful conversation with the Almighty. Talk about taking your problems to someone who can help!

Paul tells us that there are two elements to this prayer. The first is petition. In other words we are to **ask**. The Bible tells us,

> *You want something but don't get it. You kill and covet, but you cannot have what you want. You quarrel and fight. You do not have, because you do not ask God. When you ask, you do not receive, because you ask with wrong motives, that you may spend what you get on your pleasures.* - James 4:2,3

James says we are not living victoriously because we are not turning to the Lord. We quarrel, fight, kill, and covet (more on this later). We will manipulate, rationalize, and work ourselves to death.

We try everything to address our problems except the one thing that can really help . . . prayer! We don't have, because we don't ask, or because we are asking for the wrong things!

Jesus said,

Ask and it will be given to you; seek and you will find; knock and the door will be opened to you. For everyone who asks receives; he who seeks finds; and to him who knocks, the door will be opened.
- Matthew 7:7,8

This isn't that hard to grasp if you have children. Often a parent wants to help their child but knows that the child needs to learn to do things on his or her own. We want to help, but we know that the help will be seen as an infringement on our child's freedom. Sometimes our help is resented if it is given without solicitation. So, we stand back. We wait. We watch. We are ready to help as soon as we are called upon. Deep down we are hoping that our children will ask for our help. We delight to help them but we don't want to make them feel that they are incapable, so we wait. God delights when we ask Him for help.

Bruce Wilkinson tells about a fable about a Mr. Jones who dies and goes to heaven,

Peter is waiting at the gates to give him a tour. Amid the splendor of golden streets, beautiful mansions, and choirs of angels that Peter shows him, Mr. Jones notices an odd-looking building. He thinks it looks like an enormous warehouse — it has no windows and only one door. But when he asks to see inside, Peter hesitates. "You really don't want to see what's in there," he tells the new arrival.

Why would there be any secrets in heaven? Jones wonders. What incredible surprise could be waiting for me in there? When the official tour is over he's still wondering, so he asks again to see inside the structure.

Finally Peter relents. When the apostle opens the door, Mr. Jones almost knocks him over in his haste

to enter. It turns out that the enormous building is filled with row after row of shelves, floor to ceiling, each stacked neatly with white boxes tied in red ribbons.

"These boxes all have names on them," Mr. Jones muses along. Then turning to Peter he asks, "Do I have one?"

"Yes, you do," Peter tries to guide Mr. Jones back outside. "Frankly," Peter says, "if I were you . . ." But Mr. Jones is already dashing toward the "J" aisle to find his box.

Peter follows, shaking his head. He catches up with Mr. Jones just as he is slipping the red ribbon off his box and popping the lid. Looking inside, Jones has a moment of instant recognition, and he lets out a deep sigh like the ones Peter has heard so many times before.

Because there in Mr. Jones's white box are all the blessings that God wanted to give to him while he was on earth . . .but Mr. Jones had never asked.[12]

When we pray we must be specific. We must ask God for help. But not only are we told to "ask", we are also told to **do so with thanksgiving**. Let's go back to our children again. We are eager to help if we feel that our help will be appreciated. When your generosity is taken for granted, when it is something that is demanded or expected, we resist helping. I think God is the same way. When we appreciate what God has given and thank Him for what He will do, God delights to help us.

You see, it is a matter of posture. A demanding person, an ungrateful person, puts himself or herself in the position of the master who makes demands on a servant. When we are ungrateful in prayer we act like God owes us! When we act with gratitude we take the servant position. It's the difference between a child who says, "Give me this" and the child who says, "May I have this?"

When we pray we must always do so confident that God will provide what is best for us. Our job is to present our need and then trust that God knows the best way to meet that need.

I frequently have to deal with a mechanical problem at home or at our church building. I'm smart enough to know that when these problems arise I need to ask for help. Often I will stand around and watch as an expert makes the repair (who knows, I might learn something.) Sometimes I will offer my advice, "What would happen if you . . . . " and the person will turn and look at me with a look of astonishment at my lack of knowledge and then respond, "No, it is better to do it this way because then you won't: flood your house, or electrocute yourself, or remove the item that is holding up this load-bearing wall and so forth." (By the way, for the record, in these situations sarcasm seems uncalled for. It is not at all helpful.) When dealing with an expert you ought to trust the wisdom of the expert. They know best. God is the expert we turn to. We make a request and then trust His wisdom.

If God shows you something you need to do, do it. If He gives you His advice in the Bible, follow it. If there is something you need to repent of, confess it. If God tells you to "trust Him", do so.

To combat worry, we gratefully give God our problem, confident that He is willing and able to help us.

THE PROMISE

This leads us to the promise that Paul gives. He tells us what will happen if we stop worrying and instead start turning to God with the trusting attitude of a grateful child. "And the peace of God, which transcends all understanding, will guard your hearts and your minds in Christ Jesus."

Paul doesn't' proclaim that all our problems will go away. We aren't told that we will immediately understand the circumstances we are dealing with. We aren't even told that the problem won't seem to get worse before it gets better. We **are** told that the churning will be replaced with peace. If we turn to God, worry gives way to faith; anxiety gives way to a calm confidence.

But how can we have peace in the midst of the storms of life? What is it about turning to the Lord in worshipful, confident and grateful prayer that brings calm in the churning?

We find peace because when we pray in this way we are

reminding ourselves that our God is capable. It is like the old Allstate insurance commercial. We remind ourselves that we are in good hands. When we remember what God is able to do, it helps us to relax.

In prayer we remind ourselves that God knows our need and wants to help us with that need. God is not indifferent to us. He is willing to help us when we ask for His help.

Let's play this out. Let's suppose you have recently had a medical test. You haven't felt well, and you are concerned. No, you are worried. You can't sleep as you anticipate the results of the test. You know it is unprofitable, but you begin to imagine all the things the Doctor may say. You recognize the churning building inside so you look for a quiet place to spend some time with God.

In this quiet place you talk to the Father about your situation. You are honest about your anxiety and your concerns. You ask God for help. You tell Him that you know He loves you and that you trust Him. And you keep telling Him this until you believe what you are saying. Suddenly you are reminded of several things,

- The God who loved you enough to send His Son for your salvation is not going to abandon you now
- God's wisdom is far superior to anything the world can muster. You realize that this crisis is an opportunity to demonstrate trust.
- God's power can change circumstances or help us through the worst of times.
- And even if the worst-case scenario comes true (you have cancer and die) this life is not all there is. There is more to life than our present existence. It is not how long you live, but how faithfully you live.

So as a result of this time of prayer you are now able to relax. You want the test results to show that there is no problem. You want everything to be the way that is most comfortable for you. But you know that even if it doesn't turn out that way, God has good things in store for you. He knows what He is doing. He can handle it.

You've met some of these folks, haven't you? They face disease, death and all kinds of difficult circumstances not with a sense of resignation but with confidence. I began this book with the example of Dr. James Montgomery Boice. He faced death with confidence and joy.

The person who faces the future with resignation says, "There's nothing I can do about it so I guess I'll just have to live with it." These people become negative, withdrawn, and depressed. The people who face the crisis with confidence say, "There is nothing I can do, but God will do what's best and I will trust Him." This person lives without fear. They may even joke in a crisis. They face death joyfully and faithfully. And they do all this because their focus is on the Lord and not themselves or their circumstances.

PRACTICALLY SPEAKING

So here's the question? Is there anxiety that is robbing you of joy today? Does just the mention of worry cause your mind to drift to the problem that weighs heavy on your heart? Have you had trouble concentrating because of the anxiety that seems to be smothering you?

If so, it is time to do several things. First, it is <u>time to repent</u>. It is time to confess that you have been living as if God doesn't care or isn't capable to help you. Face this issue squarely. Confess your sin and ask yourself the honest question, "Do I believe or don't I?"

Second, it is <u>time to pray.</u> It is time to get alone and open your heart to the Father. Don't pretend; tell Him what you are really concerned about. Be honest. Don't stop with superficial platitudes. Make your requests known to God. And as you pray, thank Him for the faithfulness that He has proved in the past. Thank Him for His willingness to help. Thank Him for His wisdom and His grace.

Third, <u>do what you can</u>. If you are anxious about a speech, prepare diligently. If you are worried about debt, get rid of your credit cards. If you are worried about retirement, set up a 401K and begin preparing. But once you have done what you can (and should) do . . . place your confidence in the Father's love and wisdom.

And finally, <u>enjoy life again.</u> It is time to rest in His arms. It is time to leave the future with the Lord. It is time to give Him our worries so we can experience the joy that comes from grace.

Discussion Questions

1. Who is the "worrier" in your family?
2. What kinds of things are you most likely to worry about? What benefits do you see coming from this worry? What are the negative things that come from your worry?
3. What do you think is behind our worries?
4. Why is it so hard to live and pray thankfully?
5. Have you ever had a time when you experienced the peace of God that surpasses comprehension?

17

Learning to Think Like a Child of the King

Philippians 4:8,9

Two people can look at the same situation and draw very different conclusions. Some people face an obstacle in life and see it as an opportunity for growth while others see that same barrier and see it as a tragedy weighing them down. Some people see a difficult person as a challenge; others see this same person as an annoyance that will ruin their day. We all would like to discover the positive attitude that would free us to be more joyful in every circumstance.

In our last chapter we looked at Paul's instruction about the peace of God. In this chapter we will look at the second piece to the formula for living with God's peace: learning how to talk to ourselves (in that non-crazy kind of way). When we learn to focus our attention on the positive things of life, we will discover God's peace and joy.

> *Finally, brothers, whatever is true, whatever is noble, whatever is right, whatever is pure, whatever is lovely, whatever is admirable—if anything is excellent or praiseworthy—think about such things.*

Whatever you have learned or received or heard
from me, or seen in me—put it into practice. And the
God of peace will be with you. [Philippians 4:8,9]

There is a famous scene in Peter Pan. Peter is in the children's bedroom; they have seen him fly; and they wish to fly too. They have tried it from the floor and they have tried it from the beds and the result is failure. "How do you do it?" John asked. And Peter answered: "You just think lovely, wonderful thoughts and they lift you up in the air." That sentiment is a little sappy but it also contains a measure of truth. The only way to defeat evil thoughts is to learn to think differently.

Paul wrote,

We demolish arguments and every pretension that
sets itself up against the knowledge of God, and we
take captive every thought to make it obedient to
Christ. 2 Cor. 10:5

We must take charge of what we think about! We tend to believe we can't control what pops into our head. Perhaps that is true. But we can choose what we *dwell* on. In this chapter we look at two general principles that will help us think more positively.

WE ARE TO FOCUS ON WHAT IS TRUE RATHER THAN ON WHAT IS NOT

The word true can stand in opposition to many different words. Something can be true instead of false; true instead of fickle (as in a true friend); true instead of crooked (a wall that is "true"); true instead of phony (the true Messiah). So which use of "true" does Paul intend. Could it be that he means all of them? We are to spend our time thinking about the things that are accurate, genuine, and reliable. In order to do this we need to do at least three things.

First, we must become aware of the falsehoods that masquerade as truth

Before we can think about what is true we have to be able to distinguish it from what is false. We are bombarded with ideas and philosophies all the time. Some of these are conscious but many of the ideas that govern our lives are on a sub-conscious level. Our brain hears them, but we aren't really aware of it.

It wasn't all that long ago that we learned that some unscrupulous advertisers were (and maybe still are) using subliminal messages. For example, in a movie, the theatre would insert several scattered frames that might show a bucket of popcorn, an icy glass of soda, some candy. You wouldn't be able to see these frames because they would go by so quickly, but your brain would see them and immediately you'd start desiring popcorn. It was a subtle form of mind control and it is now illegal to engage in such practices.

This goes to illustrate the fact that our subconscious is receiving much more information than we realize. Let me give you some examples of what I mean.

Have you ever awakened to a clock radio and then found that all day long you were humming the song that was playing? You may not have "heard" the song but you "heard" it. Have you ever been watching a ballgame and suddenly found yourself humming the music from some Commercial? (There is nothing quite as embarrassing as a Christian mowing his or her lawn while whistling a beer commercial!)

Advertisers are very deliberate in selling not just products, but also culture. They study trends and seek to mold those trends for their financial advantage. Make no mistake; this kind of research is big business! We must not be naïve enough to think that no one would try to control the way someone else thinks.

Our minds face an assault from movies, television, theatre and even the news. These media outlets often promote values and behaviors we don't quickly see because we consider entertainment as values neutral . . .it's not.

You may remember the story of the woman who always cut off the ends of the beef roast before cooking it. Her husband didn't understand all the waste, so he asked her why she did that. She said she didn't know, that was just the way her mother always did it and mom's roasts were great!

The next time the wife was with her mom she asked her why she always cut off the ends of the roast before cooking it. Mom said that was the way Grandma always did it!

Fortunately, Grandma was still around. When Grandma was asked why she always cut off the ends of the roast she responded, "Because it was the only way I could fit it into the pan I had." Even our family and friends influence us in ways we aren't aware of.

We must work to make these messages conscious so that we can interact with them. The question is: how do we do this?

- Talk to the television and to the movies you watch (if you're in a theatre it is probably best to speak silently or quietly). Ask, "What are you trying to get me to believe?"
- Turn the television and radio off if it is just serving as background noise because you are hearing more than you realize.
- When reading (even books like this one) learn to interact with the ideas presented. Learn to ask, "Is this the way God views things?" Even some "Christian" books present ideas that are long on theory and short on Biblical basis. Take nothing for granted.
- Ask yourself why you do what you do and think the way you do. If your answer is, "it is just the way I am" take some time and try to identify WHY you are that way. What philosophies govern your thoughts and actions?
- Learn to ask newscasters, "Is there more to this story?" Try to always find out the "other side" because it usually gives a very different slant on the "truth". In the book BIAS by Bernard Goldberg, this former CBS correspondent reveals the not-so-subtle bias that exists in the news media. We must learn to listen critically if we are going to focus on that which is true rather than false.

Second, we must be intentional about pursuing the truth

Paul tells us to think about the pure (that which accurately reflects God) and to focus on the right (or the righteous . . .that which pleases God.) We don't naturally think godly thoughts. We have to work at it. In Colossians 3 we are told to "set our heart" to "set our mind" and to "get rid of" the vices of life. We have a responsibility to work at thinking and acting in a godly way.

It is like programming a computer. We must put the information in the computer before it is of any use to us. If we do not fill our minds with what is good and true, we will not be able to think about what is good and true.

Obviously, the place to start is with the Word of God. As we meditate on God's Word we are anchoring ourselves to truth that will not drift and is not subject to the whims of public opinion. But we need to do more than simply read the Bible, we must know and interact with God's Word. Here are some ideas on how we can do this?

- Make time to read and interact with the Bible daily. Read with a pencil and notebook handy to write down what you learn.
- Memorize verses of the Bible so you can have them when you need them and so they can get deep into your heart. Go into any Christian bookstore and they can show you a number of Bible memorization aids. I found a computer program that has helped me in my Bible memorization.
- Pray about what you read. When you read the Bible make what you learn a matter of prayer. For example, if you were reading Philippians 4:8,9 on thinking about what is pure, lovely, admirable, excellent and praiseworthy, you would examine your own thinking before God in prayer. You might say, "Lord, you know how much my mind focuses on the negative. You know how often my mind drifts toward lust, hate, and what is wrong with other people. You know that I am more often critical than encouraging. I repent of such behaviors. Lord, help me this day to focus on that which is good, pure, holy and positive. Help me to be conscious of the negative thoughts in my life so that I can find your deliverance from such things."
- Take notes during a sermon reflecting on what you are learning.
- Get involved in a Sunday School Class
- Read more books (like this one) that explain or interact with God's Word.
- Make it a point to ask, "What is God's perspective on this situation?"

We must be diligent and intentional about pursuing the truth.

Have you ever been on a river with a canoe or a boat? Suppose you were going to paddle upstream on the Mississippi. It would be a good challenge because of the swift current. Suppose after you had paddled up stream for a while you decided that the view was so relaxing that you would just lay back in the boat for a few minutes to enjoy the day. Let's also imagine that it was so relaxing that you took a little nap. What would happen? Before long you would be back where you started! The current in the river is active even when you are not.

This is a true picture of the Christian life. There is no such thing as static Christianity. If you are not growing toward Christ, you are drifting away from Him! We must be intentional and persistent in those intentions.

We Must Tell Ourselves the Truth

About our Nature I've said this many times in this book. We need to remind ourselves that we are created by and for God and reflect His image. But we also need to remember that we are sinners saved by grace.

The person who has a problem with alcohol, drugs, gambling, money, sex, or food needs to remember their condition. They need to remember how weak they are so that they will stay away from anything that might lead them back into their addiction. You and I must constantly remind ourselves of our addiction to sin so that we can combat pride and rebellion in our heart.

About God's Love. Yes, we are sinful people at heart, but we are also sinful people who have been saved by grace . . . by God's wonderful and undeserved gift. God cares about us. He loves us and has provided the way for you and me to be forgiven and transformed. Christ's death was a payment for our sin, and He has granted us His Holy Spirit to help us in the process of growth.

About the circumstances of Life One of the favorite pastimes of Christians is drawing premature conclusions about the circumstances of life. We conclude something is a tragedy before we even have the facts.

Suppose a family member is delayed in getting home. We begin to imagine all kinds of things. We imagine our loved one has been in an accident, or they are having an affair, or they have been abducted, or any number of other things. Our imagination robs us of our peace and our anxiety builds. In these times we must remind ourselves of what is true: our family member is late. That is the only true fact we have. Of course, we could remind ourselves that this family member is a careful driver, is responsible, and sometimes loses track of time.

Let's take another example. As you get older you find that you can't do what you used to do. Maybe you can no longer play sports. Maybe you can't drive anymore because your eyesight is bad. Maybe you are having trouble getting around because your body doesn't work as well. Maybe you have had to retire because you just can't do the job anymore. Maybe you can't seem to remember anything. At this point many people tell themselves that productive living is over. Since they can't do *anything* anymore they start to feel sorry for themselves. It is at this point that we need to tell ourselves the truth. It is true that we can't do what we used to do. But just because we can't do what we used to do doesn't mean we can't do anything! We simply need to find different things to do and different ways to get around.

Suppose you are heading out on summer vacation. You get a flat tire or have car problems. Is it really true that your vacation is ruined? No! What is true is that things are not going just the way you planned them. The vacation isn't over . . . it is just different. The truth is that sometimes these unexpected things are the most memorable and enjoyable parts of the trip.

I have officiated at a number of weddings. Lots of things can go wrong in a simple 30-minute ceremony. When these things happen (someone faints, a veil catches on fire, a microphone goes dead, the organ quits, someone says the wrong thing) it may seem like a tragedy at the time. Some people will say that this event "ruined" their wedding day. But the truth is that these are the things that set the day apart and make the day most memorable!

When we learn to focus on the truth, we will find that anxiety is replaced with peace.

We Need to Focus on The Positive Rather than Negative

Paul tells us that we should think about things that are "noble" and "lovely" and "admirable" and "praiseworthy". In other words we should turn away from dwelling on that which is offensive, dirty, and negative.

Even those outside the church understand this principle. A popular management book is called "Fish". It is a small book that tells the secrets that the Seattle Fish company. This business has learned that they can make their business fun, effective, and as a result, more profitable. The first secret to their success is the understanding that they can choose their attitude toward their work.

We can moan about our jobs. We can complain about how little we get paid. We can simply "endure" or we can choose to enjoy. We can choose to make work fun. We can choose to focus on the service we can extend, or the benefit we can provide, and we can take pride in the product we produce. It's a matter of where we choose to set our mind.

We choose the way we respond to our circumstances. We can focus on our inability, or God's great sufficiency.

The same is true with people. We can spotlight their failures or victories, their strengths or weaknesses. Paul says we should look for the good in others. We *choose* how we view other people. We need to make that choosing something we do consciously.

How much time do you spend spotlighting the weaknesses of others compared to talking about their strengths? I'd bet you spend more time on the negative than you'd care to admit. In fact, I bet if we analyzed the things we say to the people we love, we would be horrified that we speak more negative words than positive.

Paul tells us we should celebrate and spotlight people's progress rather than their failures. We should try to catch people doing things right rather than harping about the things they do wrong. We all have rough edges and we all let people down on occasion. Beating each other up over these things doesn't help anything. When we focus on the negative several things happen,

- we develop a critical spirit rather than a positive spirit
- we push people away rather than draw them closer
- we hinder unity in the body of Christ by forcing people to

choose sides rather than work together
- we are a poor witness for the gospel
- we reveal that we lack love
- we make others tentative rather than willing to risk, because they are afraid of failure and the ridicule that will follow.
- we invite others to be critical of us

What is the "up side" to a negative spirit? There is no up side! But when we are positive toward others,
- we spur people on in their efforts
- we give them courage and strength
- we build a spirit of appreciation and oneness in the body of Christ
- we find that people begin to open up to us and we discover some incredible treasure in the people around us
- people speak well of us
- people try harder and dream bigger
- conflict, churning, anxiety give way to laughter, joy and peace
- and best of all: God smiles

PRACTICALLY SPEAKING

There are many more things to say and lots more to learn. But hopefully we have enough to start working on. Let's conclude with some pointed questions. Answer these questions honestly.

1. Where do your thoughts go when you have some idle moments? Do you wallow in godlessness or are you feeding on the truth? Do you dwell on the obstacle or the opportunity?
2. Are you a negative person or a positive person? Do you build people up or tear them down?
3. Who is controlling your thinking? The media? Your friends? Your Professor? The Word of God? Which of these "teachers" has the greatest access to your mind?
4. Are you intentional about filling your mind with the good, pure, and valuable truth of God?
5. What can you do right now that would help you think God's thoughts so you can live in His joy?

I can't imagine a person who will read this chapter who doesn't need a little improvement in this area of their life. I need help in the way that I think also. Let's ask God to help us. Maybe we can help each other. We'll hate it at first, but what if when we saw the negative and destructive thinking creeping up in each other we said things like this,

- Did you make a conscious choice to be grumpy today?
- Would you call that a positive or a negative comment?
- How do you think God would view this situation?
- Do you think you may be jumping to a conclusion ahead of the facts?

I hope you get the idea. I know I could use that kind of accountability. I don't want to be a negative thinker. I want to be a godly thinker. I don't want to suck the life out of the situation and people around me. I want to infuse life into the people and circumstances around me. I want to stand for that which is pure and not cave in to that which is not. I want to choose the good, enjoy the beautiful, pursue the noble, and I want to walk in the sweetness of God's peace. Unless I miss my guess, that's what you want too.

Discussion Questions

1. What negative messages do you think come from the media around us? (News shows, talk shows, radio, the newspaper and magazines)?
2. How can we combat the negative messages from question one?
3. Can you think of some practical exercises to make your thinking more of a conscious activity?
4. The author suggests several areas where we need to "tell ourselves the truth". In which of these areas are you most liable to forget the truth?
5. If you could summarize what God is teaching you in Philippians 4:8-9 in one sentence what would that sentence be? (Don't just quote the verse . . . work to discover God's message to your life.)

18

The Secrets of Being Content

Philippians 4:10-13

There is perhaps no greater symptom of the need for joy in our society than the prevailing attitude of discontent. Look around you. People can't seem to "get enough" of anything. Professional athletes who make more in one year than many people who have good jobs could make in a lifetime, always want more. People with nice homes want bigger homes. Normal and attractive people want to alter the way they look through plastic surgery.

The gambling industry feeds off that desire to "have it all". One good bet or one lucky moment and we are told that we can be living the "good life". Of course we are not told about the risk (probability) of losing everything. We are not told that the majority of gamblers destroy their lives and the lives of their family. We are not told that most serious gamblers end up with nothing but an addiction that consumes them.

The entire advertising industry is set up to encourage and feed off of our discontent. Every commercial we watch is designed to get us to desire something we didn't desire before. These commercials are designed to dissatisfy us and make us want what the advertiser is selling.

Discontentment leads to broken homes (happiness is found in a better spouse), financial bondage (I need/want it whether I can afford it or not), rising crime rates (if I can't have what I need . . . I'll just take it from someone else), and a devastating joylessness. Discontentment makes us miserable.

In the final words of Paul's letter to the Philippians the Apostle Paul declares that he has "learned to be content". It is a state of mind that most people don't even know exists. To most people, contentment is momentary. It is something you feel during a good time in your life but it is always followed with heartache. Contentment as a settled state of mind; contentment as Paul describes it, is a rare gem. It is one final addition to his blueprint for joy. It may be the most difficult and important ingredient of all.

> *I rejoice greatly in the Lord that at last you have renewed your concern for me. Indeed, you have been concerned, but you had no opportunity to show it. I am not saying this because I am in need, for I have learned to be content whatever the circumstances. I know what it is to be in need, and I know what it is to have plenty. I have learned the secret of being content in any and every situation, whether well fed or hungry, whether living in plenty or in want. I can do everything through him who gives me strength.*
> (Philippians 4:10-13)

Paul had received some kind of financial gift from the church in Philippi. Their gift touched his heart and he is very grateful for the generosity of these believers. But Paul wants the church to understand that he has not been pining away waiting for people to send him money. His sufficiency is in the Lord and not in their ability to provide. This is contentment.

The person who lacks contentment is never satisfied. And if you are never satisfied, then you will never be able to enjoy life fully because you will almost always feel deprived. Let me give you my definition of what the Bible means by contentment: ***Contentment is a state of satisfaction anchored in our confidence in God that results in a joyful celebration of life.***

I hope this definition makes you yearn to find contentment. I yearn for it in my own life. As I have gotten older I have experienced it's wonder in greater measure. I want it to be the settled state of my life just like you do. In this passage Paul reveals four key truths.

Contentment is a Learned State

Contentment is not something that comes naturally. Paul said that he had to "learn to be content". Naturally, we are prone to,
- compare ourselves with others
- to want more than we have (remember Adam and Eve?)
- to interpret someone else's good fortune as coming at our expense
- to complain

You don't have to teach any of these things. They come naturally to us. Not so with contentment. Contentment is not natural. It is something that we must learn over time. Paul moved from this natural state of not being content to a point of true contentment. You and I can do the same thing. I suspect that Paul learned contentment gradually. In the same way, we will not just wake up one day feeling content.

We don't DO something to be content. We must develop a new perspective, a new attitude, and a deepened faith. These things cannot be bought.

Contentment is not about Possessions or Circumstances

Paul says that he had learned how to be content in good times as well as hard times. His contentment was not anchored to the circumstances of life.

> "Someone tells of a king who was discontented. In fact he was so anxious, he couldn't sleep, rest, or think. He called his wise men and asked them what he could do.
>
> One very old and very wise man said, "Find a man in your kingdom who is content, then wear his shirt for a day and a night, and you will be content."
>
> That sounded like a good idea to the king, so he

ordered some of his servants to search for such a person.

Days blended into weeks before his servants returned. "Well," said the king, "did you find a contented man?"

"Yes, sire," his servant replied.

"Where is his shirt?" asked the king.

"Your majesty, he didn't have one."[13]

Contentment is not about what you have. It is an attitude. Paul told Timothy,

> *godliness with contentment is great gain. For we brought nothing into the world, and we can take nothing out of it. But if we have food and clothing, we will be content with that. People who want to get rich fall into temptation and a trap and into many foolish and harmful desires that plunge men into ruin and destruction. For the love of money is a root of all kinds of evil. Some people, eager for money, have wandered from the faith and pierced themselves with many griefs. But you, man of God, flee from all this, and pursue righteousness, godliness, faith, love, endurance and gentleness.* [1 Timothy 6:6-11 (NIV)]

Paul reminded Timothy that we all start with nothing and we all end with nothing. You never see a hearse towing a U-Haul! When one of the Rockefeller's died his accountant was asked, "How much did he leave?" The answer was simple, "All of it."

Contentment is not tied to what we accumulate; it is about living with satisfaction one day after another. As long as we equate contentment with stuff, we will find contentment always beyond our reach.

Paul warns Timothy that when we focus on "stuff", all kinds of things happen. We become more susceptible to temptation because we find that we are more willing to compromise our principles to get what we think will make us happy. Eventually, our appetite will dictate our values rather than the other way around. Discontent inevitably leads us away from God.

It is especially hard to be content in the difficult times. We look around and see others who seem to be doing better than we are and we feel "cheated". It is hard to feel satisfied, confident and joyful when,

- others ridicule us
- when we are falsely accused
- when the medical test results are not encouraging
- when someone gets promoted to the position that we wanted (and felt we deserved)
- when our plans are suddenly changed
- when loss comes barging into our life
- when a loved one tells you they are walking away
- when a financial investment falls on it's face
- when you feel "poor" and excluded

It's tough to feel content when life is not going the way you want it to be going.

But it is just as difficult to be content in the times of plenty. When a person is going through tough times they cherish their friends, they dig deeper in their faith, and sometimes can find contentment because all that is superficial is stripped away.

Not so with abundance. When things are going well it is easy to become tied to our possessions. We begin to feel that what we have is an indication of who we are. We think the reason we are happy is because of what we have and the stuff becomes our idol. When the times of success come into our lives we may turn to "friends" based on what they "can do for us". We begin to believe that we don't "need anyone". We may become arrogant and start to look down on others.

Let's say you go out and buy a new car. It was probably more than you could afford, but it sure does feel good to drive a shiny new vehicle. But why? Deep down we feel that our new car tells others that we are successful. There is a sense in which at least for a little while (until the newer and better version of our car comes out) we feel superior to our friends and neighbors.

Paul tells us that he had learned to be content when he had much and when he had little. He was content when he was in the Penthouse and when he was in the Outhouse. When he had little he appreciated every little gift. When he had much he worked to be generous and to use his good fortune for the glory of God.

Contentment Comes from Learning to Appreciate What You Have in Christ

There is a great account in 2 Samuel about the Grandson of King Saul. His name was Mephibosheth. (Maybe his friends called him "Buck" for short!) He was crippled and instead of being killed by David (it was common practice to kill anyone from the former King's family who might be considered a rival to the throne) he was invited to David's table to eat and was given the lands that belonged to his grandfather.

When David's son, Absalom, led a coup on the throne, David was forced into exile. Mephibosheth (Buck), Saul's grandson, stayed in Jerusalem and Ziba, the manager of Mephibosheth's household, came to David with supplies and gifts and played up to the King.

When asked why Mephibosheth didn't come out to see the king, Ziba saw an opportunity to advance his own cause. He told David that his master stayed in Jerusalem because he believed he would be given the Kingship of his Grandfather Saul. (This wasn't the truth.) When David heard the words of Ziba he became angry. He felt like a friend had betrayed him. In his anger David told Ziba that everything that belonged to his master would now belong to him (In David's mind Ziba was the loyal servant, Mephibosheth was not). When the coup had ended and David was returned to Jerusalem we are told.

> *Now Mephibosheth, Saul's grandson, arrived from Jerusalem to meet the king. He had not washed his feet or clothes nor trimmed his beard since the day the king left Jerusalem. "Why didn't you come with me, Mephibosheth?" the king asked him.*
>
> *Mephibosheth replied, "My lord the king, my servant Ziba deceived me. I told him, 'saddle my donkey so that I can go with the king.' For as you*

know I am crippled. Ziba has slandered me by saying that I refused to come. But I know that you are like an angel of God, so do what you think is best. All my relatives and I could expect only death from you, my lord, but instead you have honored me among those who eat at your own table! So how can I complain?"

"All right," David replied. "My decision is that you and Ziba will divide your land equally between you." "Give him all of it," Mephibosheth said. "I am content just to have you back again, my lord!" [2 Samuel 19: 24-30]

Mephibosheth had been set up. During the entire time of David's exile he had adopted the posture of a mourner and had prayed for his safe return. His loyalty had never wavered. Ziba was a conniver. Mephibosheth had been cheated out of his land by the one who slandered his name.

David was in a tough spot. He had acted impulsively before he had checked the facts. (Admit it, it is encouraging to know that the great King also did impulsive things on occasion.) David tried to reach a compromise by dividing the land between the two men.

But Mephibosheth is not bitter, he said, "I don't care about the land. I only care about you." He understood that the greatest treasure he had was his relationship with the King. The land was inconsequential. It reminds us of the words of the Psalmist,

Whom have I in heaven but you? And earth has nothing I desire besides you. My flesh and my heart may fail, but God is the strength of my heart and my portion forever. [Psalm 73:25-26]

Contentment begins to grow when we come to understand that our greatest treasure is our relationship with the Savior. Discontent arises when we feel we have been deprived. When we understand what we truly "deserve" and compare it to what we have received in Christ, we will be able to say with Mephibosheth, "as long as we have the Savior, we have everything we need, and far more than we deserve."

Contentment is anchored to our relationship in Jesus. Paul said, "I can do everything through Christ who gives me strength." Paul had learned that whatever the situation, as long as he had the Lord at His side, He could be victorious.

How did Paul learn of God's faithfulness? He learned through the experiences of his life. As Paul faced trying times and as he trusted Christ in those times, He found that the Lord was faithful. Let's imagine what some of those times were,

- when he was in jail
- when he was being attacked by a mob
- when he was popular and everyone wanted a "new word" from the Lord
- when he counseled the troubled
- when he was exhausted from a long day of ministry
- when he was down to his last dollar
- when others slandered his character
- when he felt there was more to do than he had the energy to do

Paul learned that God loved Him in all circumstances. He learned that Christ's commitment to him transcended circumstances. He saw how faithful God was.

Contentment is found by Focusing on The Character of God

<u>We find contentment in the Grace of God</u>

No matter what the circumstance we know that we are getting better than we deserve. We deserve eternal punishment but are given eternal life in Christ. We deserve to be cast from God's presence but we are declared to be part of His family. Do you understand what a treasure this is? There is nothing . . . . nothing . . . nothing . . . that compares in value to what we have been given by God's grace. We are the richest of people because of His mercy.

Malcolm Muggeridge one of England's most articulate journalists summed up his pursuit of pleasure.

> *I may, I suppose, regard myself, or pass for being, as a relatively successful man. People occa-*

sionally stare at me in the streets—that's fame. I can fairly easily earn enough to qualify for admission to the higher slopes of the Internal Revenue—that's success. Furnished with money and a little fame even the elderly, if they care to, may partake of trendy diversions— that's pleasure. It might happen once in a while that something I said or wrote was sufficiently heeded for me to persuade myself that it represented a serious impact on our time—that's fulfillment. Yet I say to you — and I beg you to believe me—multiply these tiny triumphs by a million, add them all together, and they are nothing—less than nothing, a positive impediment— measured against one draught of that living water Christ offers to the spiritually thirsty, irrespective of who or what they are. [14]

When we finally come to realize the value of God's grace we will also begin to find contentment.

I love the scene in the classic film, "It's a Wonderful Life" when George Bailey finally realizes that all the things he had taken for granted, all the things he resented because they "kept him" from his desire to travel, were in reality the finest blessings of his life. He runs through the snow covered streets and notices and rejoices at each business. He dashes home and embraces the very ones he had yelled at earlier in the evening. He learned to see with new eyes. He came to understand what was really important.

Isn't that what we need? We need to have our eyes opened to riches of what God has given us. We need to see that the things we crave are only keeping us from seeing the treasures we have already been given.

We find contentment in the Providence of God

We also draw our sense of satisfaction from the providence of God. Our comfort comes form the fact that God is in charge. He is overseeing the events of our life and using them to deepen and develop us. God's hands are sure like a master craftsman. His chisel will not slip.

Imagine a sculptor. He begins with a block of marble. To us, it seems like nothing. But the artist, who seems to see something that we don't, begins the process of chipping away at the marble. From our perspective the chips are random and meaningless. But soon the marble begins to take form. The artist continues to chip away and before long a masterpiece is revealed.

Imagine how you would feel if you were that piece of marble. You would resent the intrusion of the chisel and feel the one who held the chisel was a cruel tyrant. But you would be wrong.

We can have contentment in the good and bad, the easy and difficult, the enjoyable and painful times of life because we trust the one who guides the chisel of circumstances in our life.

God does not make mistakes. When he is dealing with the lives of His children His actions are purposeful and loving. We can give thanks for every circumstance not because we enjoy everything or because everything is turning out the way we prefer. We give thanks because we have come to trust the character of the Master.

We find contentment in the Promises of God

We also base our contentment on the promises of God. Think about some of the promises that steady our hearts and give us perspective.

- There is a place in Heaven he is preparing for us . . . this world is not all there is (John 14:1-3)
- He will never leave us or forsake us. . . we never have to face a battle alone (Hebrews 13:5)
- He will provide for our needs . . .we are never without the resources we need (Philippians 4:19)
- He will guide us into the truth . . . When we need guidance we know that God will lead the way. (John 16:13)
- He will do in our life immeasurably more than we could ask or imagine . . . We don't have to trust only what we can see, touch, and taste. (Ephesians 3:20)

God, who does not lie, has given us His promise. Unfortunately, we live in a day when we find it hard to trust anyone. Witnesses lie in court, President's commit perjury, heads of corporations falsify documents, charlatans bilk people out of millions, and priests violate their vows and abuse children. We are left to wonder if there is anyone we can trust.

There IS someone we can trust. We can trust our Father in Heaven. There is no "shadow of turning" in Him. His character has not been diminished by the times. He is impervious to those who wish to re-define right and wrong. His standards are sure and unchanging. His promises are not empty words; they are the resolve of His heart.

Practically Speaking

Let me give you some final suggestions on how you and I can move toward contented living.

First, I hope you see that because our contentment is anchored in the character of God, <u>our first step towards contentment is to be right with Him</u>. We will never know contentment until we know the cleansing of His forgiveness and grace. And we can never know these things until we stop talking about Jesus and begin trusting Him.

I've talked a great deal about salvation in this book. That is because we cannot know joy or peace or contentment until we are right with God through Christ.

You can try to apply everything you read in this book, but if you have not really surrendered to His love, grace, and control in your life, you will not find the joy you are looking for. What you are looking for comes out of your relationship with the Savior.

Please, make sure of your salvation. Let Him begin His work in you. Receive His grace, believe His promises and trust His providence in your life. And as you turn your eyes upon Jesus, you will find "that the things of earth will grow strangely dim, in the light of His glory and grace."

Second, we need to realize that contentment is tied to our being <u>completely present in the present</u>. Discontent comes from focusing on what might have been or on what could be. Contentment comes when we start to enjoy the present. We become content as we enjoy each day for what it is rather than moan about what we imagine it could have been.

Do you see how practical this is? Instead of moaning about the fact that you don't live in a bigger home, have fun with your current home. Instead of moaning about how active your children are, enjoy being able to share those times with them. Don't miss the joy of the present by whining about what might have been. Instead of staying awake dreaming about that new car, enjoy the fact that the present one is paid for. Instead of yearning for the "new and improved", celebrate the fact that the "old and deficient" does the job. Stop looking beyond the moment and enjoy that moment!

Third, contentment comes when we understand that material things are given as tools and not as an end in themselves. Discontent (or coveting which of course is a sin condemned in the ten commandments) makes us selfish. We hoard and hide because we believe we have to have more to be happy. The contented person is generous and willing (and eager) to share because they have come to realize that honoring God is where satisfaction comes from. They use what they have to honor the Lord and in return they find contentment.

Finally, contentment comes as we grow to love Christ more completely. Too many people believe that happiness, fulfillment, and satisfaction are found in power, possessions, promotions and pleasure. But these roads lead to a dead end. There is only one road to contentment and it goes through Jesus.

Pursue your relationship with the Master with diligence. Work to know Him better. Establish your priorities in life around time getting to know the Father, Son and Holy Spirit. Stop letting other things crowd out the most important thing.

Get better acquainted with the One who loves you with an everlasting love. Because when you come to love Jesus more you will begin to enjoy the "moments of life". You will leave worries about tomorrow with the Lord and you will accept every situation as God's wise classroom for your growth and development. And when this happens you will find that in good times or bad, pleasant or painful — you can be content. And you will have found the joy you have searched for all your life.

Discussion Questions

1. If you could have anything in life, what would you like to have? Be honest. After you have answered this question, consider what your answer says about the level of contentment that exists in your life.
2. Do you agree that catalogs, commercials and advertising in general are designed to create a discontented feeling? Why do you believe the way you do?
3. Why is an accurate understanding of the gospel the foundation for the contentment that brings joy?
4. How does an understanding of God's providence help us deal with the apparent inequities of life?
5. Why does a proper understanding of grace help us to appreciate what we have . . .little or much?

Acknowledgments

A s a person tries to write a book there are many people who help them complete the task. In writing this book there are a number of people that were extremely helpful.

Thank you to the congregation of the Union Church of La Harpe Illinois. Most of what I write begins in our sanctuary on a Sunday morning. I am grateful to Pastor a congregation of people who are hungry to know the truth and eager to share that truth with others. These people have helped me to experience joy in the journey of life. As of this writing we have been together for 21 years. People often ask me why I haven't moved to a larger church. The answer is simple, "I know when I have something good!" The people of the Union Church are small town people who have a worldwide vision. Without their support I would never have begun writing.

I thank my family once again. Writing takes time away from the family. I am grateful to Maggie, Rick and Rachel for being supportive and understanding. They support me in this endeavor and cheer me on to the goal. It is wonderful to know the love of a good woman. I am a lucky man, and I know it. My children are treasures that fill my life with joy. They are both adults now and I am so proud of the people they have become. My greatest legacy in this life will not be the books I have written; it will be our children.

I extend warm gratitude to Dennis and Peg Ostrander. Dennis is the station manager at KAYP (www.kayp.org) our local American Family Radio Station. His support of my writing and the enthusiasm he and Peg showed for the early drafts of the chapters of this book spurred me on to complete the task.

I am indebted to the work of James Montgomery Boice. I didn't know Dr. Boice personally, but his life and ministry have made a huge impact on my life. He encouraged my writing in a brief conversation a few years ago. His books have instructed me and served as an example of clear and faithful exposition. I mourn his death but I also look forward to our meeting in Heaven.

Thank you once again to my friends at Xulon Press. This is our third book together. Tom Freiling and Karen Kochenberger provide encouragement and guidance in so many different ways. Their wisdom, enthusiasm and counsel have kept me on track.

I am a man who has been blessed beyond measure by a God whose love knows no limits.

Endnotes

[1] Tim Stafford, KNOWING THE FACE OF GOD (Colorado Springs: NavPress, 1996) p. 215-216

[2] James Montgomery Boice, *Philippians* (Grand Rapids: Baker 2000) p. 107

[3] Charles Spurgeon, Metropolitan Tabernacle Pulpit, Vol. 2 p. 614

[4] D. Martyn Lloyd-Jones *The Life of Joy and Peace* (Grand Rapids: Baker, 1999) p. 178

[5] Boice, *Philippians* p. 144-145

[6] Eugene Peterson, *The Message* (Colorado Springs: Navpress, 2002)

[7] D. James Kennedy, SOLVING BIBLE MYSTERIES (Nashville: Thomas Nelson, 2000) p. 199

[8] James S. Hewett, Illustrations Unlimited (Wheaton: Tyndale House Publishers, Inc, 1988) pp. 26-27

[9] © 1982 by Warren Wiersbe. From the book Be Hopeful. Copied with permission by Cook Communications Ministries. May not be further reproduced. All rights reserved.

[10] Frank Peretti The Wounded Spirit (Waco: Word, 2000) p. 84

[11] Gerald Sittser, Loving Across Our Differences (Downers Grove: IVP, 1994) p. 73 Used by permission .

[12] Bruce Wilkinson Prayer of Jabez (Sisters OR, Multnomah) p. 25-27

[13] Steve Brown Jumping Hurdles, Hitting Glitches, Overcoming Setback (Colorado Springs: Navpress, 1992) p. 162

[14] Malcom Muggeridge JESUS REDISCOVERED (Garden City, NY Doubleday, 1969) p. 77,78

CPSIA information can be obtained at www.ICGtesting.com
Printed in the USA
LVOW06s2351240914

405771LV00001B/183/P